"Why are you here? Did I invite you?"

Rachel stared at him infuriated, but Jaime only replied, "Don't you remember?"

"If I did I wouldn't be asking, would I?" she retorted crossly. "I remember going to bed, I remember you coming in here...."

"But nothing else?" Jaime was mocking.

"I'm not sure," she said reluctantly. "Anyway, you had no right to stay with me, whatever I said. You knew I had had too much to drink. I'm not used to it— I didn't know what I was doing."

"That's a pity," he taunted.

"What did happen?" she pleaded. "Did we make love?"

Jaime turned his head to look at her. 'Don't you know?"

Anger welled up in Rachel. She wanted to yell, "I don't know anything about you, Jaime Shard. I never have and I never will!"

ANNE MATHER
is also the author of these

Harlequin Presents

and these

Harlequin Romances

Many of these titles are available at your local bookseller.

For a free catalogue listing all available Harlequin Romances
and Harlequin Presents, send your name and address to:

HARLEQUIN READER SERVICE
M.P.O. Box 707, Niagara Falls, NY 14302
Canadian address: Stratford, Ontario N5A 6W2

ANNE MATHER

a haunting compulsion

Harlequin Books

TORONTO • LONDON • LOS ANGELES • AMSTERDAM
SYDNEY • HAMBURG • PARIS • STOCKHOLM • ATHENS • TOKYO

Harlequin Presents edition published May 1981
ISBN 0-373-10429-4

Original hardcover edition published in 1981
by Mills & Boon Limited

CHAPTER ONE

"Do come, Rachel. You can't possibly spend Christmas alone in London. Jaime won't be home, you know that. We wouldn't expect you to come if he was. But you know how much Robert and I would like to see you again, so do come, do come, do come...."

Rachel closed her eyes as the words echoed through her head over and over, like a relentless tattoo beating against her brain. Liz had been so persuasive, so sympathetic about her father's death, so determined that she should not spend the festive season alone in her apartment, that it had seemed churlish to go on refusing. Where was the harm, after all? Liz and Robert were nice people, and she liked them. And since Jaime spent so much time abroad, they would no doubt welcome some young company.

Rachel sighed and opened her eyes again as the lights of Durham appeared through the hazy darkness ahead of the train. Only a few more miles and they would be in Newcastle, her destination. The prospect was no longer so appealing.

Perhaps she should not have come, she argued with herself uneasily. This was Jaime's home, not hers; these were Jaime's parents. All right, so they had treated her more like a family friend than their son's—*what*? Rachel's lips tightened instinctively. Secretary? Girl friend? *Mistress?* A shudder ran over her. Whatever she had been, she was no more, so how could she talk to them as she used to? How could she discuss her plans for a future in which they had no part? It was an impossible situation. She could envisage the awkward looks, the pregnant silences, the periods of introspection, while each of them regretted the impulse that had brought them all together. And they were committed to ten days of this purgatory. It was going to be awful.

In an attempt to shake off the mood of melancholy that was settling on her, Rachel straightened up in her seat, and retrieving her handbag, extracted her compact. The compartment of the train was almost empty, so she flicked the case open, and examined her reflection in the mirror.

Her lipstick needed renewing, she decided, but apart from that, the three-and-a-half hour journey from King's Cross had not wrought any dramatic changes in her appearance. The same calm Madonna-like features gazed back at her, her dark chestnut hair thick and smooth from a center part. Her cheekbones high and lightly tinted with becoming color, her nose firm and straight, her wide mouth, with its sensuous lower lip, deceptively vulnerable. Yet the delicate conformity of those features chilled her somewhat; the slight tilt at the corners of dark-fringed green eyes only emphasized their cool remoteness. Her beauty had long since ceased to please her; the gratification that came from knowing she was attractive to men had died when Jaime proved its worthlessness; and although she still attracted male eyes wherever she went, she had learned to keep the opposite sex at a distance.

The train ambled through Durham station without stopping, and then picked up speed again between the two cities. Already the air felt fresher, colder, even within the air-controlled comfort of the compartment. It was more than two years since she had been this far north, and longer than that since Jaime first brought her to Clere Heights, and introduced her to his family. But she remembered the sharpness of the air, and the sound of the wind as it whistled around the eaves of the house, and the tumult of the waves, spuming on the rocks beneath. Clere Heights was built on the very edge of the ocean, high above the unpredictable currents of the North Sea, and there was no place in the house where one could escape its savage thunder.

Jaime's room had been at the back of the house, Rachel remembered reluctantly, overlooking the bay, that in summer could be as calm and as blue as the Mediterranean. But on winter nights the roar of the elements had been strongest here, and it took some determination for her to push away the memories her thoughts evoked now. It was all in the past, she told herself impatiently, but that didn't prevent it from hurting.

Of course his parents had known, but she had not blamed them. They were not responsible for their son's behavior, and the friendship that had sprung up between Rachel and the Shards had survived in spite of everything. Nevertheless, she could not help feeling she was accepting their hospitality under false pretenses, and if Jaime knew, she doubted he would approve.

The train rumbled ponderously over the Tyne Bridge,

and below her a ship's siren hooted mournfully from the trailing vapors of the fog that shrouded the river. The station was just beyond the bridge, a cavernous edifice, blackened from the age of steam, and presently damp, misty and heavy with the smell of diesel.

The intercity express that had brought Rachel from King's Cross pulled into the platform, and after tightening the belt of the dark red leather coat around her slim waist, she hoisted her suitcase and struggled to the carriage door. She guessed Jaime's father would have come to meet her, and dismissing the proffered services of a young porter, whose keen gaze had alighted on the graceful lissomeness of her figure, she walked as quickly as she could toward the ticket barrier.

There was no sign of Robert Shard, however, in the press of people waiting to meet the train. Tall like his son, his gray head would have been instantly noticeable, she was sure, but there seemed mostly women standing in groups, watching the discharging passengers.

"Rachel! Rachel, I'm here!"

The slightly breathless feminine tones attracted Rachel's attention as she was replacing her return ticket in the bag looped over her shoulder. Glancing around, she saw not Jaime's father, but his mother hurrying toward her, her attractive features flushed with anxiety, her ready smile breaking as Rachel saw her.

"Oh, my dear, I was so afraid I was going to be late!" Elizabeth Shard enveloped the girl in a warm embrace, bestowing a welcoming kiss on her smooth cheek. "It's quite foggy out of town, and I got stuck behind a horse trailer, and I was convinced the train would be punctual when I wasn't.''

Rachel laughed, returning the older woman's hug enthusiastically, feeling her earlier misgivings melting slightly in the warmth of Liz's greeting. "Actually, it is on time," she conceded humorously, glancing at her watch. "But so are you, so calm down. I've just walked off the platform.''

"Have you? Have you really?" Liz examined her face with a worried scrutiny, and then gave a little laugh. "Thank heavens for that. I can breathe freely again. Now— shall we get some assistance?''

Before Rachel could protest, Liz had summoned the very porter she had refused earlier, but fortunately he seemed not to notice. Picking up her suitcase and the leather travel bag containing the book and magazines she had brought for the journey, he led the way outside, and tucking her arm through Rachel's, Liz urged her to follow him.

"At least I had no difficulty in parking," she remarked as they emerged into the damp misty air, and detecting a trace of irony in her voice, Rachel wondered why. Perhaps it had something to do with Robert's not meeting her, she reflected, and hoped her visit was not a cause for contention between them.

"Did you have a good journey?" Liz asked, supervising the loading of Rachel's belongings into the trunk of the sleek gray Jaguar that was awaiting them in the station yard. "It's such a filthy night. Not at all like the day before Christmas Eve! I wonder what's happened to all our white Christmases.''

Rachel smiled and made some suitable response, and

then coiled herself gratefully into the front seat of the car. It was good to feel warm again, and when Liz came to join her, she said as much.

"Yes. It is rather chilly," her hostess agreed with a grimace. "Never mind. We still have open fires at Clere Heights."

"I'm looking forward to that," Rachel admitted, settling more comfortably in her seat, and again sensed a certain tenseness as Liz started the engine.

"So, how are you?" As if to dispel any such suggestions, Liz changed the subject. "We were so sorry to hear about your father. It must have been a terrible shock."

"It was rather," Rachel agreed with a sigh. "But it wasn't totally unexpected, you know. He had had heart trouble for a number of years."

"Yes." Liz nodded. "I remember Jaime—that is—you spoke of it when you were here before."

Rachel nodded, aware of how difficult it was going to be to avoid using Jaime's name, and added, "It's over now. It's almost four months since daddy died. And thank goodness I have my work."

"Yes." Liz slowed to accommodate traffic lights, and then went on, "You're an assistant editor now, aren't you? You must find that more exciting than secretarial work."

"Oh, I do." Rachel spoke with enthusiasm. "It means I can use my own initiative, instead of only carrying out someone else's. I find it very interesting."

"But not too hard, I hope." Liz gave her a swift glance. "You look...thinner. I hope they're not working you too hard."

Rachel smiled. "Thinner is hardly a flattering description," she commented teasingly. "You should say slimmer. Thinner implies skinny."

Liz gave a reluctant laugh. "Well, you're not that. But you're not as...rounded, as I remember."

Rachel bent her head. That was true. But it wasn't entirely due to her work or to the shock of her father's death. She had lost weight after the breakup with Jaime, and she had never really regained it.

"That's enough about me," she said now, refusing to become introspective. "How about you...and Robert? Are you both well?"

"Rob and I?" Liz spoke a little breathily. "Oh—why, yes. Yes, we're fine, thank you, Rachel. Nothing seems to bother us. Except for the occasional cold, you know. And a twinge or two of rheumatism." She moved her shoulders dismissingly. "Old age, I suppose."

"You're not old."

Rachel was quick to dispute it, but Liz shook her head. "I'm fifty-seven this year, and Rob's sixty," she declared flatly. "We're not getting any younger."

"But that's not old," Rachel argued affectionately. "Is Rob still working as hard as ever? Surely he doesn't still go to the office every day."

"Not every day," Liz conceded with a tight smile. "Since Robin joined the firm, he's taken a lot of work from his father's shoulders, and I expect eventually he will take over."

Robin was Jaime's younger brother. At the time Rachel had known Jaime, he had been at university, and she had only met him once. He was married now, she knew, and in her last letter Liz had mentioned that they had become grandparents at last. Rachel guessed they wished Jaime had been like his brother, content with running the family steel business, but an ordered life had never appealed to him.

"I suppose your granddaughter must be two months old now," Rachel murmured, needing something to say now and not quite knowing what, and Liz nodded.

"Lisa? Oh, yes." She smiled. "She's quite adorable. Her grandfather and I see a lot of Robin and Nancy."

Rachel acknowledged this, wondering how Jaime's brother had reacted to the fact that she was to spend Christmas with his parents. Did that account for Liz's occasionally taut countenance, the sudden air of enforced courtesy, so out of keeping with her normal uninhibited chatter? She was getting the distinct impression that all was not well at Clere Heights, and taking the bull by the horns, she said, "Is something the matter, Liz? I want you to be honest with me." And as the older woman started to protest, she added, "I know you invited me here, and I am grateful, really, but if it's causing any problems with the family—"

"With the family?" Liz interrupted her impatiently. "Rachel, what possible problem could your coming here create with the family?"

She shook her head vigorously, and taking the opportunity, Rachel plunged in again. "I'd just hate for you to feel that you've committed yourself, and you can't change your mind," she said. "I mean, I can easily stay at a hotel—"

"I wouldn't hear of it." Liz sounded as if she meant it, and Rachel sighed.

"But something's wrong, isn't it? It's not Robert, is it? I must admit, I expected it would be he who came to meet me—"

"Jaime's home."

Liz broke in on her attempted explanation with flat deliberation, and Rachel felt all the blood drain out of her face.

"What—what did you say?" she echoed faintly, but she knew without Liz repeating it. She had said that Jaime was home, and the shock drove the strength from her body.

"I'm sorry, darling, but it's true." Liz was hastening on with her explanations now. "We didn't know he was coming. How could we? It was totally unexpected. He only arrived the day before yesterday—"

"You should have told me." Rachel only managed to articulate the words with difficulty. "You should have let me know. I would have made other arrange—"

"He wouldn't let us," Liz exclaimed helplessly. "And why should you, anyway? You were invited. He was not. And if he hadn't been shot, he wouldn't be here—"

"*Shot!*"

Rachel hadn't thought it was possible for her to feel more shocked, but she did. She turned in her seat, gazing in horrified fascination at Jaime's mother, and Liz quickly told her what had happened.

"He's all right," she assured her urgently, while Rachel fought to control the overwhelming instinct she had to grasp Liz by the shoulders and shake the information out of her. "It's a nasty wound, but he'll survive. He's fortunate not to have been injured before this, the places they send him! God knows, he was lucky to escape with his life."

Rachel endeavored to assimilate what Liz was saying, but her mouth was dry, and there was a beading of perspiration dewing her forehead. Jaime had been shot, she told herself incredulously. Someone had tried to kill him, but miraculously, he had escaped serious injury. How had it happened? Where had he been shot? And how long would it take for him to recover?

"I know it must be a shock to you, Rachel," Liz was going on sympathetically. "You can imagine how we felt when he turned up on Tuesday afternoon. They flew him home from Masota on Monday, and I think they would have preferred him to spend a few days in hospital in London, but you know what Jaime's like. He flew to Newcastle on Tuesday morning, and arranged for a rented car to bring him home."

Rachel expelled her breath heavily and forced down the sense of panic inside her. This was ridiculous, she chided herself angrily. She was behaving like an idiot. Why should it matter to her what happened to Jaime Shard? He meant nothing to her any longer, and of a certainty, she meant nothing to him. Why get upset just because he was hurt? He deserved to suffer for the way he had made her suffer; and Betsy, too, come to that. Perhaps fate was kinder than she thought. Perhaps retribution came to everyone in time.

"You...you mentioned Masota," she said now, her brain working furiously as she tried to decide what she should do. Obviously she could not stay at Clere Heights now, whatever Liz said, but conversely, she could hardly demand that she turn the car around and take her back to the station tonight.

"Yes, Masota," Liz agreed, accelerating as the outskirts

of the city fell away behind them, and the fog enveloped them in its ghostly embrace. "You know where it is, don't you? It's one of those central African republics." She sighed, having to slow her speed again as visibility was reduced. "There was a coup. You may have read about it. That's why Jaime was in Kamsuli." She shook her head. "It was one of those awful coincidences. The camera team was caught in an ambush laid by the government forces, would you believe? He spent four days in a prison hospital before they would let him go."

Rachel moistened her lips. "And... and how is he?"

"All right, I suppose. Subdued." Liz grimaced. "Wouldn't you be?"

Rachel managed to nod her head. "I'm sorry. For... for your sake, I mean. It must have been a terrible jolt, him just turning up like that."

"With his leg all stiff, and walking on crutches?" Liz added fervently. "My God! I thought he had had it amputated at first. My blood went cold!"

Rachel could imagine their reactions, and she thought how typical it was of Jaime not to give them any warning.

Choosing her words carefully now, she said, "You must see, Liz, I... I can't stay as we intended. I mean... I just can't!"

"Why can't you?" Liz turned to give her an appealing gaze. "Rachel, my dear, I know how you must feel, believe me! But, you must try and understand our feelings, too." She shook her head. "That's why I came to meet you, and not Rob. I thought—foolishly perhaps—that you might take the news more... naturally from me."

"Well, I would—I did!" Rachel made a helpless gesture.

"Liz, I appreciate what you're trying to do, I really do, but—"

"If you leave, Jaime will leave, too," Liz declared flatly, and Rachel caught her breath.

"What do you mean?"

Liz hesitated. "When we told him—Jaime, that is—that you were coming, he guessed how you would react when you found out he was here."

I bet he did, thought Rachel tautly, but she didn't say it.

"He knew if we forewarned you of his presence, you wouldn't come." She put her hand gently over Rachel's fingers, tightly linked together in her lap. "My dear, it is Christmas. Couldn't you allow for these...unexpected circumstances?"

Rachel turned her face away. "What did you mean when you said, if I go, Jaime will go, too?"

"That's what he said," averred Liz unhappily, and Rachel felt a bitter sense of injustice kindling inside her. This was also typical of the way Jaime used people. He knew he could not stop Rachel from leaving by any normal methods, but by threatening to leave himself he had effectively tied her hands. How could she go, knowing she would be depriving his parents of their son's company during this season of the year, particularly when they saw him so infrequently? His home was in London, and most of the time he spent in England, he spent there, in the luxury penthouse apartment with its magnificent view of the city. It was only rarely he made the journey north, and it was pure misfortune that he should have come to them now, just when Rachel had planned to visit there.

Rachel bent her head now, not knowing how to answer the older woman, and Liz made a sound of frustration. "Look, darling, I know this has all come as a shock to you, and you're probably thinking we're unreasonable in hoping you will stay, but is it so impossible?" She sighed. "After all, it's not as if you're going to be alone with Jaime or anything. Robin and Nancy and the baby are coming tomorrow, and on Christmas Day we're having quite a party!" She waited for Rachel's response, and when she said nothing, she added, "I'm sure you'd enjoy it, Rachel. Imagine how we'll feel if you let Jaime drive you away."

It was hopeless! Rachel pressed her lips together tensely, and sought a way out, but there was none. No matter how she strove to find an answer, she persistently came up against the wall of Jaime's ultimatum, and she could imagine the bitterness it would evoke if he insisted on returning to London. Particularly when he had been hurt and had turned to his parents for help.

She drew an uneven breath. Somehow she was going to have to make the best of it, at least, until Christmas was over. She could not let the Shards down, not now, not after they had been kind enough to open their home to her. It was not their fault that Jaime had arrived and disrupted all their arrangements. And as it evidently was his leg that was injured, might he not spend a good deal of the time in his room anyway? He would need to rest to recover his strength, and surely after all this time, she was not afraid to face him.

"All right," she said at last, making the fateful decision. "I'll stay, Liz. Over the weekend, anyway. After that—we'll see."

"You won't regret it, darling!" Liz's relief was palpable. "Oh—I don't know what I'd have done if you'd refused." She allowed a nervous little laugh to escape her. "I so much want us all to enjoy this Christmas!"

Rachel forced a small smile. "I hope you won't be disappointed," she commented, unable to keep the dryness out of her tone. "And, please—don't expect too much."

"A reconciliation, you mean?" Liz shook her head. "No, my dear. We don't expect that."

"Good." Rachel's response was fervent, and she turned her head away again to stare blindly through the misting windows. She could never forgive Jaime, she thought, *never*! And the prospect of the next few hours filled her with apprehension.

In spite of the fog, the journey was over all too soon as far as Rachel was concerned. The forty or so miles between Newcastle and Rothside, the nearest village to Clere Heights, was accomplished in a little over an hour, and it was only a quarter to nine as Liz drove between the stone gateposts that marked the boundary of the Shard's property. Rachel remembered that the drive that led to the house wound between hedges of thick rhododendrons, that in early summer were a mass of purple flowers. But at this time of the year the glossy leaves were drooping and wet with the mist that rose thickly from the ocean. The crunching sound of wheels on gravel was muted by its drifting vapor.

It was a reluctant relief to see the house looming up ahead of them. Lights gleamed through uncurtained windows, throwing shafts of illumination across the graveled forecourt, and as the car ground to a halt the heavy oak door swung wide to reveal Robert Shard's broad figure.

With the mist shrouding the upper floors of the house, Rachel could only imagine the long-leaded windows baying out above the front door, and the clinging creeper that covered the walls and gave them a pinkish tinge. She could see the wide bay windows on either side of the door, and glimpsed the leaping flames from the open fire Liz had promised her, but although she told herself she had had no alternative, she couldn't help the certain conviction that she should not have come here.

"Rachel, my dear!" Robert Shard had descended the shallow steps and crossed the forecourt to swing her door open. "Welcome to Clere Heights! I'm so glad you made it. Isn't it a vile night?"

"I was almost late," his wife commented, climbing out at the other side of the car. "The fog's really thick." She smiled across at Rachel. "It's just as well you weren't flying up. I'm sure the airport must be closed."

As Rachel got out, she heard the muted thunder of the ocean, and her heart quickened. Returning Robert's kiss with a nervousness she tried hard to disguise, she admitted that the weather wasn't at all seasonal, and then thanked him for inviting her, through lips stiffened, she insisted, by the cold.

"It was a pleasure," Robert Shard assured her warmly, drawing back to study her face. "I suppose Liz has told you, we've got an unexpected visitor. I guess it came as something of a surprise."

An understatement, thought Rachel tautly, but she managed to disguise her misgivings. "I feel something of an...interloper," she offered, glancing around at Jaime's mother. "I'm sure you'd all enjoy yourselves better if I...was not here."

"Rubbish!" Robert wouldn't hear a word of it. "We've been looking forward to your visit, and hearing all about what's been happening to you. Isn't that so, Liz?" And at his wife's nod, he continued, "But go along inside now. Are your suitcases in the trunk? Good. I'll get them."

Rachel hesitated, but Liz came around the car to join her, tucking her arm through the girl's and urging her forward. "Come along," she said. "I'm sure Maisie's got supper all ready and waiting. I expect you could do with something to eat."

In truth, Rachel had never felt less like eating, but she could hardly say so, and she accompanied Liz into the hall of Clere Heights, feeling sick with apprehension. Where was Jaime? Was he waiting for them in the comfortable sitting room, that the Shards used most evenings? Was he in bed? She faced the coming confrontation with a feeling close to dread, and she wondered if Liz had noticed she was trembling.

"Take off your coat," said Liz as they stood beneath the attractive chandelier that hung above the wide, square hall of the house. Paneled in a dark wood, but highlighted by the pale gold carpet underfoot, the hall was as big as any of the rooms Rachel had known in her father's house, and the staircase that wound around two walls was broad and stately, and heavily carved. An enormous bowl of pink and cream roses occupied a prominent position on the oak settle that stood at the foot of the stairs, and their perfume mingled with the dampness from outside as Robert carried in her luggage and shouldered the door closed.

Rachel was removing her leather coat as Maisie Armstrong, the Shards' housekeeper, came bustling through the door beneath the curve of the stairs that Rachel knew led to the kitchen. She had heard the heavy door slamming, and her thin face broke into a smile when she saw their visitor. "Well, well. It never rains, but what it pours," she exclaimed, beaming at Rachel. "What a night to arrive, to be sure. You'll be thinking we have nothing but bad weather up here."

"I know you don't," Rachel assured her, smiling and handing over her coat. "How are you, Mrs. Armstrong? You're looking well. The weather doesn't seem to disagree with you."

"Ah, Maisie was born and bred to it," Robert remarked, making for the stairs. "Come along, Rachel. I'll show you to your room before supper. I'm sure you'd like a few minutes to wash your hands and comb your hair."

Blessing his understanding, Rachel nodded eagerly. "If you don't mind," she said, looking anxiously at Jaime's mother, and Liz made a deprecating gesture.

"Of course I don't mind," she exclaimed, but there was a faint trace of tension in her expression. "Come down to the sitting room when you're ready."

"Thank you."

Rachel nodded, and suppressing the desire to hurry, she followed Robert up the stairs.

A landing circled the hall on two sides, with corridors running in either direction to the two wings of the house.

Built at the end of the last century, when economy of dimensions was not at a premium, Clere Heights was a rambling, spacious building, with two floors above ground level, and one below. The second floor rooms were smaller than those on the first floor, meant in the initial instance to accommodate a full quota of servants, but Rachel knew from her previous visits that these were seldom used now. The Shards, who had lived in the house for the last thirty-five years, had made certain modifications—adding central heating and bathrooms and updating the electrical system— but the character of the place had not been altered, and Rachel had always been happy here. But that was because she had been with Jaime, she thought tightly now, closing her mind to the coming encounter.

Robert led the way along the corridor that gave access to the south wing of the house, and opened the door into a spacious apartment that sprang to life when he switched on the lamps. The soft green carpet underfoot was reflected in green and gold curtains and a matching patterned bedspread, and Rachel recognized the dark oak furniture from her visit two years ago.

"Remember it?" inquired Robert, setting her suitcase on the ottoman at the foot of the square bed, and Rachel nodded mutely, too overcome to speak. "We thought you'd like to be in here," he added, depositing her holdall on the bed. "Take your time and acclimatize yourself. Maisie's supper won't spoil for a few minute's waiting."

"Thank you."

Rachel's gratitude was evident in the unusual brightness of her eyes, and Robert hesitated a moment. "You don't change, do you, Rachel?" he murmured thoughtfully, giving her a rueful smile. "You're still the beautiful enigma, aren't you? The only girl I ever knew who beat Jaime at his own game. I guess that cool exterior drove him to distraction. I only wish he'd met you before Betsy got her claws into him."

This was too close to the bone, and as if he knew it, Jaime's father turned away. "See you soon," he said, raising a hand as if in apology, and closed the door swiftly before she could respond.

Left alone, Rachel drew a deep breath before surveying her domain. She still felt weak and somehow defenseless, and her own reflection in the long wardrobe mirrors didn't help. It had been a mistake to wear dark colors, she decided. The dark brown silk shirt and the matching pants above long suede boots had looked fashionably businesslike back in London. Now they looked drab and unfeminine, robbing her face of all color, and accentuating the hollows in her cheeks.

Still, she had no time to change now, and carrying her toilet things into the adjoining bathroom, she quickly washed her face. Her skin felt cold, but inside she felt as if she was burning up, and she lifted one of the yellow hand towels and held it to her face for a few minutes, staring into the haunted green eyes that confronted her. *Dear God, how am I going to go through with this*, she asked herself silently, and then thrust the towel aside before emotion got the better of her.

She had believed she was alone. She had never dreamed that the running water might have provided a screen for someone to enter her room undetected, and when she first glimpsed the dark figure, propped in the open doorway to the bathroom, she started as if she had seen a ghost. But it was no ghost who straightened at her involuntary gesture, who regarded her through narrowed mocking eyes, and she felt as if a sudden blow had just been delivered to her solar plexis.

"Hello, Rachel," he greeted her equably. "I thought it would be easier if we got this over in private. I'm sorry if I startled you, but I didn't like to interrupt your evident absorption in your appearance."

CHAPTER TWO

His SARDONIC WORDS had a steadying effect, reminding her of their last encounter. He had been mocking then, and scathing, too, and violently angry, although he had tried hard to control it, and a feathering of anticipation ran over her skin at the memory of how it had ended.

"What do you want, Jaime?" she inquired now, making a display of leaning close to the mirror again, smoothing a delicate finger over the curve of her eyebrow. "I would have thought any contact we have to have could be more suitably expressed in the presence of your parents, and I see no reason for us to exchange anything more than the time of day."

She spoke coolly, controlling the tendency her voice had to quiver a little, and felt quite pleased with her efforts. He should not imagine their previous relationship gave him any prior rights where she was concerned, and it was better to make her position clear right from the start.

"You think that, do you?" Jaime's voice was low and flat, devoid of expression, concealing his feelings. "So we're to behave like strangers, are we?"

"We are strangers," she retorted, realizing she could not go on avoiding looking at him. "I told you. I never knew you. Now—if you don't mind—"

She moved then, as if to go past him, but he was standing squarely in the doorway, and her downcast eyes could not avoid the sight of his booted feet, set slightly apart, with the narrow base of the walking stick that he favored on his right.

Her eyes moved upward almost involuntarily then, over the cream-colored corded pants that enclosed his hips like a second skin, over the dark green shirt he was wearing, the neckline unbuttoned to reveal the brown column of his throat, to the swarthy features of his lean dark face that she remembered so well. She was a tall girl herself, but he had always been taller, easily six feet, with a lean, muscular body that owed its hardness more to the tough life he led than to any particular prowess in physical sports. He was not a particularly handsome man. Like his body, his face had a toughness that denied simple good looks. But he was attractive—how attractive she knew only too well, and the hooded depths of his eyes, and the sensual twist of his mouth had an appeal that was purely magnetic. She had felt that magnetism once, she could even feel it at this moment, but now she knew the selfish nature that lay behind that sexy exterior, and she despised herself for allowing even a trace of his charisma to disturb her.

"Will you let me pass?" she demanded now, fixing her gaze on the central button of his shirt. "I want to put on some makeup and brush my hair, and your mother and father are waiting for their supper."

Jaime made no move to accommodate her. "Aren't you going to ask how I'm feeling?" he inquired, using his free hand to massage his hip. "Don't you want to know how it happened, and whether they got the bullet out?"

"I really don't see that it matters to me one way or the other," Rachel returned callously, hardly aware of what she was saying in her urgency to get away from him—from being alone with him—from this impossible situation. "Your mother explained all I needed to know. She told me you got away with it, as usual. You always had the luck of the devil!"

"Damn you, Rachel!" His harshly expressed denunciation brought her head up with a jerk, and she stared tautly into his angry brown eyes. "Have you any idea how bloody painful it was dragging myself in here? Just so that you shouldn't be embarrassed! And you stand there and tell me you don't care! You...little hypocrite!" He used a word then that Rachel would never care to repeat. "I should put you over my knee and give you the thrashing you deserve!"

Rachel quivered, but she refused to be intimidated. "I think you might find that beyond your capabilities," she retorted with a determined attempt to meet him on his own terms, and then winced in pain when his hard fingers fastened on her forearm.

"Don't you be too sure," he muttered, but she was alarmed to see the sallow cast of his features beneath his swarthy tan. He had not been lying when he said the effort of coming in here had drained him, and in spite of her angry bitterness, compassion stirred.

"Don't you think this conversation has gone far enough?" she suggested quietly, making no concerted effort to free herself. "I'm sorry if I sound unfeeling, but I've just had a long journey, and I'm tired, and I didn't know I'd have you to face at the end of it."

"You're tired!" he grated, bearing his weight on the stick as he moved nearer to her. "You're sorry if you sound unfeeling!" His mouth tightened ominously. "My God, do you think that's sufficient recompense for the way you're treating me?"

"Jaime, listen—"

"No. You listen! To me!" He jerked her toward him as he spoke, bringing her close enough to be touching him, her thigh brushing his uninjured leg. "I didn't come in here to quarrel with you or to beg your sympathy. I came because I knew it was going to be difficult for you, for both of us, and I wanted to...smooth the passage." He made a sound of derision. "But you don't want it that way, do you? You want to keep me at bay, to erect all those old grievances you've managed to perpetuate against me, to create a situation where it's impossible for us to behave normally with one another." His eyes blazed angrily. "Oh, I know you refused to answer my calls, and you didn't acknowledge any of my letters, but I thought—I really thought—we might be able to talk to one another here—"

"Well, you were wrong." Rachel could not let that go unchallenged. For the first time she tried to get away from him, but in spite of his injury, he was still a lot stronger than she was, and by struggling with him she was only making the situation more volatile. "Jaime, we have nothing to say to one another," she exclaimed, and then froze into immobility when he dragged her arm across his body and pressed her hand deliberately against his right leg.

"Feel it!" he commanded thickly. "I want you to feel it."

Rachel averted her eyes quickly from the disturbing violence in his. But rather than promote another outburst, she flexed her fingers tentatively against the corded cloth. Beneath the dark material of his trousers, she could detect the taut ribbing of the bandages, and sensed the heat of his flesh increasing to meet hers. "Well?" he muttered. "Can you feel it throbbing like a bloody pounding pulse? Believe me, I wouldn't be here if I didn't think we still had something to say!"

"Jaime—"

Her use of his name was not a plea for remission, but when she tilted her face up to his, his tormented expression was almost her undoing. Dear God, she thought dizzily, no one could disrupt her carefully controlled emotions like Jaime could, and for an insane moment she wanted him to touch her. She swayed weakly as her head swam, and her breasts pressed briefly against his chest, but then Liz's voice from the foot of the stairs called irresistibly, "Rachel! Darling, are you coming?" and cold reason replaced the heated urgings of her senses.

She did not have to ask Jaime to release her. He turned as his mother spoke, his lean face taut and brooding. "Don't worry," he said. "I won't embarrass you!" He then walked with evident difficulty out of her room.

Downstairs Robert had poured drinks, and Rachel accepted a cocktail gratefully, hoping the alcohol would calm her nerves. She had only had time to apply a little lip gloss and brush her hair, and she hoped that the Shards had not noticed her state of agitation.

"I wonder whether Jaime intends to join us," Liz said at

last, after Robert had asked Rachel about her journey, and received only monosyllabic replies. She gave the girl an apologetic look. "Dr. Manning actually suggested that he should spend some time in bed to allow his wound to heal, but you know what—I mean—well, Jaime wouldn't listen." She offered an embarrassed smile. "Er, perhaps you ought to go and see what he's doing, Rob," she finished appealingly. "We can't keep Maisie waiting indefinitely."

"All right."

Robert got up from his seat beside Rachel on the couch and, with a good-natured grimace, left the room. In his absence Liz offered Rachel another drink, and after she had refused, said, "You're not worrying about this, are you, darling?" She sighed. "I know it can't be easy for you, but after all, you and Jaime are civilized people. You can meet as old...acquaintances, can't you?"

Rachel concentrated on the clear liquid in her glass. "If...if that's what...Jaime wants."

"Oh, I'm sure it is." Liz was fervent. "I think he may be glad of the opportunity to, well, repair the damage. Oh, not for any personal reasons, but simply because he would like to heal the breach."

Rachel could not answer her, not least of all because her own preconceived ideas were in shreds. She had thought she could handle Jaime. Now she wasn't so sure whether she could handle herself. And the knowledge that he still had the power to disturb her was terrifying.

"He's not coming, after all." Robert breezed back into the sitting room with a distinct air of relief. "He says he'd rather have supper in his room. He's got a little pain, I think, and he doesn't feel like making the effort to come downstairs.''

"Oh!" Liz bit her lip and looked uncertainly down into their guest's taut face. "Well, but what about Rachel? Doesn't he want to see her? To say hello?''

"He asks to be excused this evening," Robert explained as Rachel started to make her own protestations. "He says he'll see her tomorrow—which I'm sure will be time enough for both of them," he concluded with another grimace. "Now, shall we eat?''

The meal was served in the intimate dining room that overlooked the cliffs at the back of the house. Tonight, of course, the curtains were drawn, and the only evidence of their proximity to the ocean was the persistent murmur of the sea on the rocks. The fog had reduced sound as well as visibility, and its muted cadences were low and resonant.

The food, as always, was excellent, but Rachel ate little, making the excuse that she had had a sandwich on the train. "I expect my appetite will improve with all the fresh air I'm going to get," she murmured, breaking the protracted silence, and Liz smiled her understanding.

"I think you need time to relax and get used to us again," she declared as Maisie served their coffee. "Don't worry about anything. It will all work out. You'll see.''

It was a relief, nevertheless, to escape to her room later. Closing her door, Rachel wished ardently that there had been a key, but there wasn't, and she could hardly jam a chair under the handle. What possible explanation could she give Liz and Robert if they discovered her in such a predicament? And besides, if Jaime was in pain, he was unlikely to come to her room again tonight.

Someone had turned on the electric blanket on her bed, and after a cursory wash and a cleaning of her teeth, Rachel unplugged it before climbing wearily between the warm sheets. It was deliciously warm and comfortable, and with the distant murmur of the sea from the other side of the house, she endeavored to relax. But she couldn't forget that the last time she had stayed at Clere Heights, she had not slept alone, and the knowledge that Jaime was only a few yards away across the corridor filled her with apprehension.

EVENTUALLY SHE SLEPT, and although her sleep was shallow and punctuated with turbulent nightmares, she awakened feeling at least partially rested. Outside the fog seemed to have given way to a brighter morning, and after watching the play of light between the heavy curtains at her windows for several minutes, she at last thrust back the covers and went to investigate for herself.

As she had suspected, the mist had lifted, and the view from her window encompassed the whole of the garden at the front of the house and the village of Rothside in the distance. Although the trees were bare now and the lawns had lost their lambent greenness, the thick hedges were dense and sturdy, with here and there a budding sprig of holly to provide a splash of color.

The village lay below them, its roofs gray tiled and solid, with the spire of the church just visible above a cluster of poplars. The road to the village ran beyond the barrier of rhododendrons and wound its way down between fields that Rachel remembered as being pastureland. Now, however, they had been plowed and left to turn their dark furrows to the blue sky, ready for sowing when the frosts of winter were over.

It was all much as she rememberd it, she thought unwillingly, admitting that until now she had not realized how sharply it had remained in her memory. The house, the village and the tussocky cliffs sloping down to the river estuary where the Roth spilled its waters into the North Sea.

She shivered suddenly as the coolness of her room struck through the thin satin of her nightgown, and was starting back to warm herself beneath the covers when there was the lightest of taps at her door. She stiffened for a moment, and then, realizing that Jaime would be unlikely to knock and announce himself, she opened her mouth to call, "Come in!" The handle turned and Maisie's head appeared.

"Oh, you're up!" she exclaimed, opening the door wider to reveal the small tea tray in her hands. "I thought you might still be sleeping, and Mrs. Shard said not to disturb you if you were."

Rachel relaxed. "I was just reacquainting myself with everything," she admitted, taking the tray from her cagerly. "Hmm, I could just do with a cup of tea. Especially yours, Mrs. Armstrong."

"Indeed!" The housekeeper sounded skeptical, but she looked pleased, and Rachel perched on the side of the bed, setting the tray beside her.

"Is...is everyone up?" she asked, raising the wide-rimmed china cup to her lips. "What time is it? My watch seems to have stopped."

"It's a quarter to nine," replied Maisie chattily, plainly disposed to linger. "Oughtn't you to put on a dressing gown or something? You'll be catching your death in that flimsy thing."

Rachel smiled. "Well, I was beginning to feel a bit cold," she admitted. "But your tea has warmed me up beautifully."

"Mmm." Maisie pulled a wry face. "Well, as long as you're sure." She twitched the fringe of the bedcover into position, and then added, "Mrs. Shard is downstairs taking tea in the morning room while she opens the mail, but Mr. Shard isn't up yet, and neither is Jaime."

"I see." Rachel caught her lower lip between her teeth.

"That was a rare old business, wasn't it?" Maisie went on. "Jaime getting shot like that and being brought home on crutches." She moved her shoulders expressively. "My, my, you should have seen his mother's face when he limped into the house."

"I...I can imagine." Rachel's blood quickened at the thought of it.

"Yes, well, he came to the right place," Maisie opined firmly. "It's only right that he should come home and be looked after by people who care about him."

"Of course." Rachel wondered if this was a subtle criticism of her.

"Of course Mrs. Shard was worried about that, what with you coming and all," the housekeeper continued. "But I said to her, I did, this is Jaime's home, I said, and Miss

Williams won't expect you to consider her feelings at a time like this.''

"Thank you, Mrs. Armstrong." Rachel put down her cup. "That was delicious." She moistened her lips. "Er, will you tell Mrs. Shard I'll be down in fifteen minutes?"

"Yes, miss." The housekeeper picked up the tray again and moved toward the door. "You, er, you haven't spoken to Jaime yet, have you? He's in his room just along the hall, if you'd like to go and have a word with him. After you're dressed, of course."

Rachel kept her smile in place with difficulty. "I expect I'll see him later," she declared stiffly, and the housekeeper looked disappointed.

"I'm sure he'd like to see you, Miss Williams," she persisted. "And it is Christmas Eve, you know. The season of peace and goodwill."

"Thank you, Mrs. Armstrong." Rachel's dismissal was unmistakable this time, and with a little shrug the housekeeper left her, evidently feeling she had done what she could to repair the damage.

With her departure Rachel rose purposefully to her feet again and padded into the bathroom. The night before she had paid little attention to her surroundings, but now she took time to admire the rose and cream tiles that circled the bath, and the fluted glass shower with its pinewood door. The bath beckoned, but time dictated a shower, so she turned on the tap and stepped beneath its steaming cascade.

Her hair got wet, but she had brought a hand dryer with her, and its smooth style was easily restored. Then, after examining the contents of her suitcase, she dressed in a pair of jeans and a long-sleeved cotton shirt. Boots completed the outfit, which acquired a simple elegance on her slim body, and applying only the lightest of makeup, she left the room before she lost her nerve.

In the carpeted corridor outside she hesitated for a moment, counting the doors to Jaime's room. His door was half open, as if inviting her investigation, but she was not tempted. She doubted he had asked Mrs. Armstrong to intercede on his behalf, but she had no intention of getting involved with him, whatever kind of pressure was brought to bear.

Liz greeted her cheerfully when Rachel entered the morning room a few moments later. As the housekeeper had said, Jaime's mother was absorbed with her mail, and Rachel walked over to the long windows, gazing out in silent admiration at the gray-flecked waters of the bay. Beyond a stone-pillared terrace, sloping lawns fell away almost to the cliff's edge, and the seaweed-strewn teeth of the rocks below were just visible, constantly washed by the ever moving tide. On summer days it was possible to swim from the rocks, and there were deep pools where one might find crabs and other shellfish, but although the sky was clear this morning, the sea would be cold as ice. Its distant thunder reached her as it sucked at the base of the cliffs, the rocks providing a natural protection for the more porous ridges of limestone.

Turning back to the table, Rachel seated herself and picked up the morning paper lying beside her. She flicked through it idly until Maisie put in an appearance and asked her what she would like to eat.

"We've got kidneys and sausages, or kippers, if you'd prefer them," the housekeeper suggested approvingly, but Rachel only shook her head.

"I think…just toast and coffee," she conceded regretfully. "I'm afraid I don't have a good appetite."

"Then we'll have to see if we can change that, Maisie, won't we?" Liz remarked, looking up from her bank statement. "I seem to remember you used to enjoy your food, Rachel."

Rachel colored then. "That was a long time ago, Liz."

"Not so long," Liz retorted firmly. "Didn't you use to share Jaime's bacon and eggs the last time you were here?"

His name came more naturally, and although Liz looked slightly appalled afterward, Rachel forced herself to respond without hesitation. "I was younger then," she murmured, pulling a wry face. "I have to watch my figure these days."

"Nonsense! Let us do that for you!" remarked Robert's amused tones, and Jaime's father came into the room, broad and comfortable, in a navy wool dressing gown. He bent to kiss his wife's cheek, and then squeezed Rachel's shoulders in passing before settling himself in the seat beside her. "So, you're looking more relaxed this morning. Did you sleep well?"

"Very well, thank you." Rachel saw no reason to tell them of her restless night. "And thank you for your kind words. It was a pretty compliment."

"Nothing less than the truth, I do assure you," Robert replied gallantly, picking up one of her hands from the table, and raising it to his lips. "Hmm, you smell delightful.

What is it? Something to drive us poor males mad, I'm sure."

Rachel giggled. "It's Charlie actually," she admitted, as he let her draw her fingers away. "And you're an old flatterer. I don't know what Liz must think of you."

"Oh, I'm too old now to try and change him," remarked Liz dryly, but she and her husband exchanged a knowing smile.

"You'll never be too old," he retorted affectionately, and then looked up at Maisie and gave her a wink. "I'll have the same as usual, if you don't mind," he told her. "Oh, and remind Andy I want to speak to him later about those canes in the greenhouse."

"Yes, Mr. Shard." Maisie nodded. "Shall I take Jaime's breakfast upstairs, do you think? Or is he likely to be coming down."

Liz looked uncomfortably at her husband, and he shrugged his shoulders almost imperceptibly. "I ... think perhaps you ought to take it upstairs," Liz conceded at last. She glanced awkwardly at Rachel. "You don't mind, do you, darling? He's not being deliberately rude. It's just—"

"I don't mind at all," Rachel averred, only too willing to put off the moment when she would have to face Jaime in his parents' presence, and with a sigh of relief Liz gave Maisie her instructions.

"It's a lovely morning, isn't it?" Rachel offered as the housekeeper left the room. The last thing she wanted was to lose the rapport they had recovered earlier, and as if sharing her feelings Jaime's father took up her words.

"Perhaps you'd like to walk down to the village with me

later," he suggested. "I've got a bottle of rare old Scotch whiskey for the vicar to sample, and I want to call at the garage for a couple of new plugs for the Rover."

"Rob!" His wife looked slightly scandalized. "You're not going to offer Mr. Conway some of that stuff Jaime brought you, are you?"

"Why not?" Her husband was unrepentant. "It's good whiskey. And you know as well as I do that old Conway enjoys a wee dram!"

"I know, but—" Liz shook her head at Rachel. "What would you do with him? Anyway," she sighed, "if you get drummed out of the church, don't blame me."

"They'd have to get me in there before they could drum me out!" retorted Robert with a grin. "Stop worrying, woman. Conway and I understand one another. And he plays a fair round of golf."

Rachel smiled. She had always envied Jaime his parents. Her own mother had died in a car accident soon after she was born, and she had been brought up by her father's older, unmarried sister, who had come to share her brother's home on his wife's death. When Aunt Catherine died Rachel was already fifteen, and old enough to take over the running of her father's house, and her own ambitions to do well at her A levels and go on to university had been squashed by family circumstances. Not that her father had ever deliberately stood in her way. But she had known she could not leave him, and in consequence, she had left school at sixteen, and after a year at a secretarial college had taken a job in the typing pool of an independent television company. That was how she had met Jaime, how it had all started, and she determinedly turned her thoughts aside from the memories it evoked.

Liz had already had her breakfast; like Rachel, she had had only toast and coffee, and leaving Robert to his plate of bacon and kidneys, the two women adjourned to the living room. Like the morning room, this room also was at the back of the house, and Rachel seated herself on the wide banquette that circled the long jutting bay window.

"Now...." Liz pushed the letters her husband had not wanted to see away into the small bureau, and added several cards to the collection already hanging around the mantelpiece. Unlike the sitting room, there was only an electric fire in here, but the efficient heating system banished any sense of chill. "Let me see what I have to do."

"Can I help you?" Rachel would be glad of the diversion. The last thing she wanted was to be sitting around aimlessly when Jaime eventually decided to put in an appearance.

"Well, you could get me one or two things at the store if you're going down to the village with Rob," Liz considered. "He hates going in there, you know. It's such a gossipy place. And if they've heard that Jaime is home, Mrs. Dennis will be dying to ask questions."

"All right." Rachel doubted they would remember her, and even if they did, she was not perturbed. "You make out a list, and I'll do your shopping for you. And afterward, I'm quite willing to help around the house."

Liz smiled. "You're a sweet girl, Rachel, and I'm very fond of you." She touched her cheek gently with a probing finger. "I'm so sorry Jaime hasn't even had the good manners to come and speak to you. And I will give him a piece of my mind when I have the opportunity."

"Oh, no. Don't! I mean—" Rachel broke off in embarrassment. "Really, I prefer it this way. Honestly. He...he and I have nothing to say."

"If you insist." But Liz still looked slightly doubtful. Then, dismissing her momentary solemnity, she gave another smile. "Andy is installing the tree in the hall this morning. Perhaps you could help me dress it before Robin and Nancy arrive."

Rachel displayed an enthusiasm she was far from feeling, and Liz bustled away to see Maisie, to find out what was needed from the village. Left alone, Rachel gazed out pensively at the sea gulls wheeling above the heaving waters, and wondered rather apprehensively how Jaime's parents would introduce her to their daughter-in-law.

She was lost in thought when a voice broke into her reverie. "Well, hello, Miss Williams! It is Miss Williams, isn't it? You know it's so long since we met, you'll have to forgive me if I'm confusing you with someone else."

Rachel swung around to face her tormentor, and gazed up resentfully into Jaime's dark mocking face. He was standing just inside the doorway, a sinister Machiavelli in a black shirt and black pants, his dark hair smooth and brushing his collar at the back.

"I suppose you think you're very amusing, don't you?" she demanded tautly. "If this is your idea of saving me embarrassment, then don't bother."

"Ah, but that was last night," remarked Jaime annoyingly, using his stick to walk heavily across the carpet.

"And you turned me down. So you can hardly blame me if I try to protect my own interests."

"Didn't you always?" retorted Rachel angrily, turning back to her contemplation of the view, and then stiffened instinctively when he approached the window seat and lowered himself down onto the banquette beside her.

"What a vindictive tongue you have, grandma," he taunted, glancing over his shoulder to see where she was looking. "Reliving the halcyon days of the past?" He propped his cane against the wall. "I seem to remember we spent one memorable afternoon down there."

"I don't recall it." Rachel's mouth compressed. Then she said, "I thought you were supposed to be resting. Mrs. Armstrong was going to serve you breakfast upstairs."

"And so she did," said Jaime carelessly. "Only I didn't feel particularly hungry, and naturally I felt honor bound to come and offer you felicitations."

"You needn't have bothered!"

"No. But my parents don't know that, do they?"

"I'm surprised you care." Rachel was behaving badly, she knew, but she was overwhelmingly aware of his thigh only inches away from hers on the cushioned seat, and the muscled length of his legs splayed carelessly beside her. "In any case, I...I'm going out soon. Your father and I are...are walking down to the village. So you could have saved yourself the trouble."

"Could I?"

He turned his head to look at her, and the blood rushed helplessly into her face. He was so close she could feel the warmth of his breath upon her cheek, and sensed the intent

scrutiny from between his long, dark lashes. They were the
only incongruous feature of an otherwise profoundly masculine visage, and she remembered teasing him about them,
and stroking her finger over their curling softness....

"Jaime, please—"

The intenseness of her tone was a source of irritation to
her, but she couldn't help it. He knew exactly what he was
doing, taunting her like this, and while her brain insisted that
it shouldn't matter to her how he behaved, her senses responded in a totally different way. He had always had this
effect on her, right from the very beginning, and it was this as
much as anything that terrified her now.

"What are you afraid of?" he asked, and she hated him
for his arrogance. "Why are you trembling? Do I threaten
that sterile little world you've built around yourself?" His
lips twisted. "Or do I remind you of the fun we used to
have before you became so bloody sanctimonious?"

"Before I discovered you were married, you mean?" Rachel choked, getting abruptly to her feet, needing the self
assurance that came from being able, physically at least, to
look down at him.

"Okay." Jaime shrugged his shoulders indifferently,
leaning back against the window with an indolence that
both disturbed and infuriated her. "So you've said it. It's
what you've been wanting to say ever since you got here.
Well, now I've given you the opportunity."

"You don't care, do you?" Rachel was incensed.

"Was I supposed to?" Jaime's eyes were hard.

"Don't you care about... about anything but your own—
your own—sexual gratification?"

Jaime's mouth assumed a mocking tilt. "That's a good old-fashioned way of describing it, I guess." One dark brow quirked upward. "But I have to say, you seemed to enjoy it, too."

"You—you—"

"Cad?" Jaime pressed his weight down on the cane and got to his feet beside her, immediately reducing her advantage. "That's another good old-fashioned expression. As you seem to be hooked on out-of-date attitudes."

Rachel clenched her fists. "You . . . bastard!"

"Better." Jaime's smile was malicious. "There may be hope for you yet. If you allowed a little more of the real Rachel Williams to emerge, we might find ourselves with a three-dimensional person again, instead of a cardboard cutout."

"I don't have to listen to this—"

"Why? Am I getting too close to the truth?"

The sound of footsteps approaching across the hall stilled any response Rachel might have cared to make, and by the time Liz entered the room, she had put the width of the hearth between her and Jaime, and was apparently engrossed in reading the cards on the mantel shelf.

"Oh—you two have met, have you?"

Liz's reaction was one of relief, although she glanced from her son to Rachel and back to her son again with a doubtful expression marring her attractively aging features.

"We've been having a most interesting conversation," Jaime remarked, shifting his weight with evident discomfort, and his mother shook her head impatiently, indicating the seat behind him.

"Do sit down," she exclaimed, anxiety coloring her tone. "You really should rest more, Jaime. Dr. Manning says it takes time for flesh to knit together."

Jaime pulled a wry face, but he did sink down onto the window seat again with some relief, and glancing in his direction, Rachel knew a pang of guilt at her own obduracy. She had not even asked him how he was feeling, and although she despised herself for feeling that way, she knew she was still concerned about him.

"So—" Liz forced a lightness she was evidently far from feeling "—has Rachel told you about her promotion, Jaime? She's an assistant editor now. Isn't that exciting? Who knows, she may produce her own programs one day."

"I hardly think so," murmured Rachel deprecatingly, and Jaime's cynical eyes probed her embarrassment.

"She doesn't have the right disposition," he remarked, addressing his mother, but evidently speaking for Rachel's benefit. "Her ideals are too rigid. She doesn't move with the times. Producers have to be modern in outlook, malleable in intent; they have to *feel* for their subject, and make allowances for human error. And also, they need to be capable of distinguishing between truth and fabrication."

"And be sexually aware!" exclaimed Rachel, unable to prevent the bitter retort, and Jaime inclined his head mockingly.

"That, too, of course," he murmured with heavy sarcasm, and Rachel longed to wipe the smug expression from his face.

CHAPTER THREE

"OH, WELL—" Liz licked her lips a trifle nervously, as if afraid she had accidently stirred up the very hornet's nest she had wanted to avoid. "I suppose we all have our opinions, don't we?" She cast an appealing glance in Rachel's direction. "I should have known better than to speak of it in my son's presence. Producers are not his favorite kind of animal."

"It's all right." Rachel had herself in control again, and regretted her momentary lapse and any embarrassment it might have caused the older woman. "Fortunately...fortunately, we work for different television stations. Our methods are...different."

"Well, I'm sure we all wish you success in your career," declared Liz warmly, giving her son a reproving look. "It's good to know a woman can succeed in a man's world. Generally, they seem to regard us as intellectual morons."

"Am I missing something?"

To Rachel's and Liz's obvious relief, Robert Shard's appearance was well timed. He came into the room behind his wife, arching his bushy gray brows at his son, and instantly alleviating the tense atmosphere.

"Oh, we were just discussing Rachel's work," Liz ex-

plained quickly, changing the subject before he could inter-
vene. "What time are you leaving? Rachel says she'll get me
one or two things from the store while you're at the garage."

"I see." Robert looked thoughtfully at his son, apparently still assessing the situation, and Liz gazed imploringly
at Jaime, entreating him not to rekindle the subsiding hos-
tilities.

"I think I'll go up to my room," he said, responding to
her silent appeal. "I've got some work to do, and Robin
won't be here before lunch, will he?"

"Not before three," his mother acknowledged eagerly.
"I, er, I'll have Maisie fetch you some coffee later. Is there
anything I can get you?"

Jaime got to his feet with his father's assistance and subjected Rachel to a momentary appraisal. "No," he said, and
once again she felt he was speaking primarily to her. "I
guess I've got everything I need." And with a tight smile,
he walked with difficulty through the door.

Robert waited until the sound of his son's labored ascent
of the stairs reached them, and then shook his head. "He
seems...morose," he murmured in a low tone. "Subdued.
Do you think he's all right? You don't think he's holding
anything back from us, do you? I had Manning give him a
thorough examination, and as far as he could tell, the
wound in his thigh is the only injury."

Liz pressed her lips together. "I'm sure he's all right,"
she assured her husband soothingly. "He, well, I suppose it
was bound to come as something of a shock, seeing Rachel
again." She caught her lower lip between her teeth, and
then added hopefully, "Robin will be here this afternoon,

and I know he'll be delighted to see his brother. And Jaime hasn't even seen his niece.''

"It's my fault, really," said Rachel with a heavy sigh, and ignoring Liz's automatic protest, she went on, "Jaime and I—we had an argument. I'm sure you'd all feel a lot better if I left.''

"I won't hear of it." Robert spoke adamantly, and coming toward her, he took her by the shoulders. "Now you listen to me, young woman. *We* invited you here, and that's an end of it. If Jaime chooses to go and get himself shot, and lands up here without word of warning, that's not our fault, and it's not yours.''

"I don't suppose he chose to get shot," Rachel murmured mildly, but Robert only gave her a gentle shake.

"You're staying," he said, glancing around at his wife. "Isn't that so, Liz? So go and put on your coat, or whatever it is you wear to keep warm, and we'll be on our way to the village.''

Rachel expelled her breath unsteadily. "All right.''

"Good." Robert let her go. "And don't be too long. I don't walk as fast as I used to.''

The walk to the village was invigorating, and Rachel felt herself begin to relax as soon as they were away from the house. With the wind whipping her hair into her eyes and the frosty air bringing color to her cheeks, she let the anxieties of the last few hours leave her, and gave herself up the enjoyment of the day.

"You've been down here before, haven't you?" Robert asked as they climbed the stile to take a shortcut across the field, and Rachel nodded.

"With Jaime," she said, deliberately bringing his name into their conversation, and Robert watched her face as he helped her down onto the field path.

"That must be a good two years ago now," he murmured, setting the pace.

Rachel said, "Two and half years nearly," as she quickened her step to accommodate him.

"Two and a half years!" Robert shook his head. "It doesn't seem that long, really—at least, not to me. So you must be—what? Twenty-one now, twenty-two?"

"Twenty-three, actually," admitted Rachel with a small smile. "We're none of us getting any younger."

"Twenty-three!" Robert grinned. "I wish I was twenty-three again. So Jaime must be thirty-two now, mustn't he? He is nine years older than you, isn't he? I forget."

"Thirty-two," Rachel agreed, pushing her hands deeper into the pockets of her coat. "I've known him...almost five years. Or anyway, it's almost five years since we first met."

"At the studios," remarked Robert thoughtfully, and Rachel nodded. Somehow she didn't mind talking like this with Jaime's father. Perhaps because she knew there was no bias on either side.

"But you work for a different studio now, don't you?" he inquired, turning to look at her. "Didn't Liz say you'd got some promotion?"

"Well, yes. But I changed studios two years ago—"

"After the breakup?"

"Yes."

"Pity about that." Robert moved his broad shoulders regretfully. "Your changing jobs, I mean. I thought you liked working for London Westward. Surely you could have continued as you were."

And risked the chance of running into Jaime at any hour of the day or night, thought Rachel, shivering in spite of herself. *Oh, no!* That she could not have borne. Particularly not in the beginning when she had been hurt and confused, and hopelessly vulnerable.

"Isn't that the vicarage over there?" she asked now, pointing across the field, and Robert respected her evident desire to change the subject.

"Yes. That's old Conway's country seat. Are you coming with me to see him, or would you rather press on?"

"Oh, I think I'd rather carry on, if you don't mind," replied Rachel, unwilling to get involved in further explanations with the vicar, who had been here since before she and Jaime had been involved with one another, and Robert acquiesced and said he would meet her half an hour later at the garage.

But when Rachel arrived at the garage, which was situated just off the main street of the village, she found her escort had not yet arrived. The only people there were a boy busily employed in the job of changing the tire on an old Land Rover, and a young man who crawled out from under a car he was repairing on her arrival, and asked if there was anything he could do to help her.

Even in the oil-smeared overalls he was wearing, he had an attractive appearance, and because it was a relief to meet someone who had no influence on her life, Rachel responded to the admiring smile he gave her.

"I'm looking for Mr. Shard, actually," she admitted, glancing around her. "He's not arrived yet, has he? I'm supposed to meet him here."

The young man put down the wrench he was holding and folded his arms. "You're waiting for... Mr. Shard. From Clere Heights?"

"That's right." Rachel weighed the shopping basket on her arm, and looked around for somewhere to deposit it. "He said he would meet me here at—well, five minutes ago, really. But obviously the vicar's delayed him."

"I see." The young man looked over his shoulder. "Would you like to wait in the office then, Miss, er—"

"Williams," she replied dryly. "And yes. If you don't mind, I would prefer to wait indoors. It's sunny, but it's very cold."

"Okay. Come this way."

With a casual gesture he took the basket from her and then led the way across the yard and into a cozy, if rather untidy, office, adjoining the main body of the workshop.

"This is my dad's garage," he explained as he set her basket down on the overflowing desk and switched on the electric heater. "I'm Terry Marshall, and I run the place for him."

"Hello." Rachel smiled, taking the seat on the upright chair he offered her. "I've never been in here before. Have you lived here long?"

"Just all my life," he admitted with a grimace. "But you don't live here, do you? I've never seen you before, or I would have remembered, believe me!"

Rachel laughed. "Thank you."

"No, seriously, you're not Robin's wife, are you? And I know you're not Jaime's."

"No." Rachel sobered. "I, well, I'm just a friend of the family, that's all."

"Here for Christmas?"

"Yes."

Terry acknowledged this with a thoughtful grunt. "I thought a girl like you wouldn't come from around these parts."

Rachel recovered her composure. "I'm sure the girls around here wouldn't appreciate your saying that." She saw the boy watching them from across the yard. "Is that your brother?"

"No. His name's Billy Hughes. He's an apprentice. I'm teaching him the tricks of the trade."

Rachel nodded, and then saw to her relief that Robert was approaching up the narrow lane that led from the main street. He grinned when he saw her, and came striding across the yard, looking sheepish.

"I know, I know, I'm late," he exclaimed, after bidding good-morning to her companion. "But he would insist on opening the bottle, and how could I refuse a drop?"

"I expect Liz would have an answer to that," Rachel retorted wryly, and accompanied them into the workshop as Robert explained why he had come.

"Maybe I'll see you again some time," Terry commented as they were leaving, and Robert glanced at Rachel with drawn brows.

"Maybe," she agreed, picking her way carefully across the nuts and wrenches littering the spot where the boy was changing the wheel, and then exchanged a helpless look with Robert as they walked back down the lane.

"You've made a conquest," he remarked, taking the basket from her, and she moved her shoulders dismissively. "I suppose you're used to it," he added. "You don't need me to give advice."

Rachel colored. "We talked while I was waiting," she replied flatly. "He seemed harmless enough."

"Well, I wouldn't advise you to get involved with him," said Jaime's father dryly. "He thinks he's the local Lothario."

"I thought he might be." Rachel shrugged. "Don't worry, Robert. He's not my type."

"I'm glad to hear it," Robert declared comfortably, and she wondered why she sensed a certain air of satisfaction in the way he said it.

At lunch Jaime joined them, and Rachel, fresh from her walk in the open air, thought how pale and dark eyed he was looking. She knew he had been working by the slightly abstracted air about him, but his pallor was unnatural, and she guessed his injury was troubling him.

Still, he made an effort to behave normally with his mother and father, and they were obviously relieved by this demonstration of equanimity. He even responded to Rachel's polite inquiry as to the state of his health without sarcasm, but his assurance that he was feeling much better did not quite ring true.

When the meal was over, Liz suggested that she and Rachel attend to the tree that Andy, Maisie's husband, and gardener-cum-general handyman about the place, had put up in the hall. It looked green but totally bare at the moment, and Liz was keen to have it dressed before her younger son and his family arrived. She had already brought the box containing all the tree deocrations down from the second floor, and Rachel was more than willing to find herself occupied for the rest of the afternoon.

Robert disappeared outside, having said he had matters to attend to with Andy, and as Maisie soon summoned Liz to advise her in the kitchen, Rachel was left to dress the tree alone. She didn't know where Jaime had gone. She guessed he had probably returned to his writing, and therefore she was surprised when he appeared from the library.

"Reference," he said by way of an explanation, holding up the book he held in his hand. "I see you've been abandoned. Do you need any assistance?"

"From you?" Rachel couldn't prevent the tautness of her tone, and Jaime expelled his breath wearily.

"Yes, from me," he agreed flatly. "It was an innocent suggestion, no more. But forget it. Obviously you'd rather not."

The words "Yes, I would" hovered on Rachel's tongue, but she bit them back, telling herself that she owed it to Liz and Robert to be civil at least. Instead she swallowed her indignation, and said stiffly, "If you'd like to help, of course you can. I...I just thought you might prefer to rest your leg."

Jaime looked skeptical at this. "Don't you start," he exclaimed. "I can look after myself." He put down his book on the chest and looked around. "What do you want me to do?"

Rachel moistened her dry lips. "You could...sort out the

decorations," she offered, pulling the stepladder Maisie had supplied close to the tree. "I . . . I wouldn't have thought this was your scene, really. Don't you usually spend Christmas out of the country?"

Jaime squatted down on the floor as she fixed the ornamental star to the top of the tree. "Revolutions invariably start at the most unsociable times of the year," he conceded. And then, looking up, added, "We've never spent Christmas together, if that's what you mean."

"I know that." Rachel descended the steps carefully. "Do you think that looks all right? Or should I change it for an angel?" she asked, looking up at the tree, because it was safer than looking at him, and he grimaced.

"The star looks very nice," he assured her dryly. "Come and look at these colored ornaments. What do you want next?"

Controlling the impulse to put as much space between them as was humanly possible, Rachel knelt down beside him, looking at the tree decoration in his hands. It was a silver ring with a velvety red and silver harlequin suspended from it, and she did not have to invent her gasp of pleasure.

"Oh, isn't it pretty!" she exclaimed, putting out her hand to touch, and then withdrawing it again quickly. "I—I've never seen anything quite like it before."

"It is attractive, isn't it?" remarked Jaime thoughtfully. "I brought a dozen of them back from Hong Kong about five years ago. I was sent there to report on the plight of refugees from Vietnam—"

"I know." Rachel interrupted him tensely, and he cast her a sidelong glance.

"Of course." He frowned. "You worked on that story, too, didn't you? It was your first month at LWTV."

"I only typed the story," retorted Rachel stiffly, picking several of the harlequins out of the box beside him, and standing up. "I'll hang these next." Then, forcing herself to remain calm, she asked, "What else is there?"

Jaime watched her attaching the ornaments to the branches for several minutes, his eyes following her progress up and down the stepladder as she pulled it around the tree, and then with a shrug he applied himself to his task again, pulling out several streamers of colored tinsel and a box of crackers.

"There you are," he said, leaning back on his hands, his injured leg stretched out in front of him, and Rachel approached diffidently, studying the things strewn around him.

"I think I'll use these first," she said, bending to pick up a collection of colored glass trinkets he had unpacked earlier. They were small and delicate, shaped like lanterns, fruit and huge frozen teardrops, and she admired them silently, avoiding his eyes. "Does your mother put all these things on the tree. There seems an awful lot."

"Just use what you think is necessary," said Jaime mildly. "I suggest you take the ladder, and I'll handle the lower branches. I'm sorry if that sounds ungallant, but I don't think I could make the steps right now."

"There's no need for you to get up," Rachel protested, looking at him then. "Honestly, I can do it. I wasn't hinting or anything. I was just—"

"I'm not an invalid," retorted Jaime shortly, turning onto his good knee and pushing himself upright, keeping his other leg straight as he did so. "You see. No problem. Now, what would you like me to do?"

Rachel was uncertain, aware that, standing, Jaime was far more intimidating to her. While he was sitting on the floor she had felt she could handle the situation. Now she was not so sure.

"You'd better have some of these," she said, handing over the glass ornaments she was holding. "I'm sure you know what to do."

"I used to think so," he commented dryly, and she hastily climbed the ladder before he could say more.

They were working in what was, to Rachel, a rather uneasy silence when Jaime's mother appeared. She came bustling into the hall, glanced rather absently at Rachel on the stepladder, and then halted abruptly when she saw her son around the other side of the half-decorated tree.

"Jaime!" she exclaimed. Then, looking at Rachel again, she said, "Well, isn't this nice? I didn't realize you were helping, Jaime."

"I don't know that I am," he remarked with lazy humor. "But I'm trying...and that's what really matters, isn't it?"

His mother held his amused gaze for several seconds, and then shaking her head, she transfered her gaze to Rachel. "Well, it docs look nice, darling," she began, only to break off with an exclamation, "The lights! Rachel, you haven't fixed the lights. Oh, my dear, they should have been fixed first."

"Oh, no!" Rachel sank down weakly onto the top step of the ladder and hunched her shoulders. "I didn't think about the lights. Where are they?"

"Well, they're in this box somewhere," said Liz, rummaging among the tinsel and streamers still overflowing from the box her son had unpacked. Over her bent back, Jaime caught Rachel's attention and grimaced, and an unwilling smile tilted her lips as Liz emerged triumphant. "Here they are!" she exclaimed, displaying the container in which resided a string of tiny ornamental bulbs. "I wonder what you should do."

"We'll fix them," declared Jaime, taking the box from her unresisting fingers. "I guess it won't matter if they're put on in the middle for once. Leave it to us, ma. Rachel's an expert at balancing on the ladder."

"Are you, Rachel?"

Liz looked up at her inquiringly, and the girl pulled a wry face. "Hardly," she confessed, ignoring Jaime's mocking expression. "But, don't worry. I—we'll—handle it."

"Oh, good." Liz was evidently bent on some business of her own, and after assuring herself that they could cope, she hurried upstairs, saying she was going to check on the bedrooms.

"Okay." Jaime pulled the string of lights out of the box as Rachel carefully descended the ladder. "Now, you hold that end, and we'll see how long this cable is."

"All right."

Rachel took the length of cord he offered and held it firmly while Jaime examined the remainder. There were at least three dozen light bulbs, all with fluted glass shades and composed of every color Rachel could imagine.

"I think if you can attach this one behind the star at the top of the tree, we could then divide the rest equally,"

Jaime said consideringly. "Here." He handed it to her. "Can you do that?"

"I can try," said Rachel with a grimace, now in possession of two lengths of cable, and slightly bemused by the cluster of lights at her feet. She was so afraid she might step on one accidentally, and she knew from experiences at home that one broken bulb could fuse the whole string.

"Take it easy," said Jaime beside her. "You go ahead. I'll hold them up for you."

"Thank you."

Rachel half turned, but she was nervous, and as she did so, several of the bulbs spilled from her grasp. They tumbled onto the bottom step, right where she was going to put her foot, and losing her balance on one leg, she had to quickly find somewhere else to stand.

She chose to go backward, forgetting Jaime was behind her, and only as her foot descended on his did she realize it was his injured leg. He gave a muffled oath, and stepped backward himself, and his sudden movement threw her completely off balance. She felt herself falling, and tried to prevent it by groping for the steps, but all she grasped was air before she cannoned into Jaime, who had no chance of saving himself. They fell together in a tangled heap of electric cable and colored bulbs. Rachel cracked her head on the floor, and lay there stunned for a few seconds. Jaime fell beside her, with her flailing limbs half-imprisoned by the weight of his body, his head faring a little better as he used his arms to save himself.

"Dammit!" he muttered, raising himself on his hands beside her and looking down into her shocked pale face.

"Are you all right? Did I hurt you? Hell, I'm sorry. I'm not much use with this bloody leg!"

"Your leg...." Rachel swallowed with difficulty, and her tongue came to circle her lips. "I'm sorry. It was my fault. You must be in agony!"

"Oh, I am," he agreed, but she suddenly realized he was not speaking of his bullet wound. Their proximity was having an effect on him, and in the darkening emotion in his eyes she saw the inherent danger. He had made no move to get up, and she could feel the muscles of the leg imprisoning hers, and as she turned her head she could smell the warmth of his body from the open neck of his shirt. He was totally aware of her, as she unwillingly was of him, and when she realized what he intended to do, she twisted wildly beneath him.

But he used his hand to hold her face still for him, ignoring the clawing protest of her fingernails. He covered her lips with his in a swift hard kiss that demanded a response, and when she refused to give it, he drew back to look down her broodingly.

"Little Miss Frigid!" he taunted tormentingly, and when she opened her mouth to spit her contempt at him, he bent and kissed her again.

She realized her mistake at once. This time she was unprepared for it, and her lips were parted to denounce him, emotion of another kind trembling in her throat. But one emotion was much like another, she discovered, as she fought to get away from him, and the thin line between love and hatred was as difficult to define. His lips were firm and determined, possessing hers with a knowing expertise that sapped her strength and weakened her resistance. There was urgency and hunger in his kiss, and a deepening passion that assaulted her senses and set her blood surging wildly through her veins. No one but Jaime had ever kissed her this way, so sensually, so sexually, making her intimately aware of her own body's needs, so that when his tongue invaded the moist sweetness of her mouth, she knew a wanton desire to surrender....

At this point however, Rachel rebelled. Her earlier feeble attempts to escape him had only quickened his ardor, but now she kicked out wildly, uncaring whether she hurt him or not. One booted foot connected with his ankle, and her knee drove upward with vicious intent, and as he muttered a savage oath and tried to evade her, she twisted herself free and got to her feet.

The door chimes that rang almost at the same moment brought her around with a start, her hands groping desperately to smooth her hair. She thought for a moment they might be ringing in her head, her heart was pounding so violently, but as Jaime propped himself up on his elbows, his dark face taut and pain wracked, she knew she had not imagined it.

"Saved by the bell," he remarked bitterly, and she put a nervous hand to her throat. "Go on," he added. "Answer it. Or someone may think something is wrong."

Rachel looked at him unhappily, biting her lips, twisting her hands together. "Are... are you all right?" she pleaded, troubled by his harrowed countenance, and he moved his shoulders with hard-eyed indifference.

"Does it matter?" he asked, not trying to reassure her.

"For God's sake, open the door! Our ... *business* ... can be pursued at some other time. There won't always be interruptions, believe me!"

Rachel quivered. "Why can't you leave me alone?"

"Because I'm unscrupulous—your words, not mine—or have you forgotten?" he remarked flatly, as the chimes pealed again.

"Can you answer that, Rachel?"

Liz appeared at the top of the stairs, looking somewhat flustered, and Rachel could delay no longer. With an apologetic wave of her hand, she hurriedly opened the door, and then stepped back in some embarrassment as Jaime's younger brother shouldered through the door.

"Hey, it's freezing out there," he protested, brushing past her to dump a folding pram and a cot in the middle of the floor. Then he saw Jaime and grinned. "My God! What are you doing down there? Playing electricians!"

Jaime brushed the trailing length of lights aside and made an effort to get up. But his leg was evidently hurting him more than it had before, and he sank back with a grimace, obviously disgusted with his own weakness.

"Here—" Robin gave him a hand as a young woman appeared in the open doorway, carrying a baby in her arms, and he swung around to face her as Jaime reached for his cane.

It was then he saw the girl still hovering by the open door, and he did a swift double take. "Rachel! As I live and breathe!" He exclaimed, giving his brother a sudden half-disbelieving glance before going toward her. "Rachel!" He bent and bestowed a less-than-brotherly kiss on her parted lips, before murmuring softly, "What have you been doing to him?"

"Robin, can you take Lisa, please?"

A slightly peevish voice interrupted them, and Rachel drew away from him at once, and went toward the young woman carrying the baby.

"Let me," she offered, holding out her arms, and although Nancy was evidently loath to hand her baby over to a stranger, she must have decided it was the lesser of two evils.

"Can't you close the door, Robin?" she exclaimed, after he had rescued two bags that were sitting on the step, and with a sheepish grimace, he slammed it behind him, just as Liz came down the stairs.

In the warmth of greetings that ensued, Rachel looked down at Jaime's niece, sleeping peacefully between the folds of a woolen blanket. The tranquil features were Liz's in miniature, but the fairer skin was evidently Nancy's. Robin's wife was a natural blonde, with the plump good looks that often followed a pregnancy. That she was also used to occupying center stage was evident, too, and Rachel suspected she resented anyone else usurping her position as the Shard's daughter-in-law.

When a hand descended on Rachel's shoulder, she started nervously, turning her head indignantly away from Jaime's. "It suits you," he remarked. "You ... and a baby." His mouth thinned. "Perhaps I should have made you pregnant."

Rachel's mouth trembled. "As you did Betsy?" she whispered coldly, and winced as his fingers bit into her fine bones.

"Contrary to your sordid little speculations, I was not responsible for Betsy's pregnancy," he snarled in an undertone. "And if you had half a brain in your head, you'd know it!"

Rachel pressed her lips together tightly. "Poor Betsy!"

Jaime said an obscene word that only she could hear, and moved stiffly away as his mother came to take the baby from Rachel.

"Have you been looking at your niece, darling?" she asked her son playfully. "Isn't she just the most beautiful baby you ever saw?"

"She's female," remarked Jaime flatly, his rigid features eloquent of some inner torment he was suffering, and Liz looked troubled. "I guess I'm no judge of females," he added mockingly, and Robin conferred a knowing stare on Rachel before she could look away.

CHAPTER FOUR

IT WAS THE EARLY HOURS of Christmas morning before Rachel got to bed. As always, Jaime's parents wanted to attend the midnight service at the village church, and Rachel, Robin and Nancy accompanied them. Jaime was excused on grounds of his injury, but Rachel doubted he would have come in any case. He had retired to the library with Robin and his father after dinner, and when Robin reappeared to beg a sandwich for supper, he announced that Jaime had gone to bed.

"He said something about working," he remarked dejectedly, seating himself beside his wife on one of the sofas in the sitting room. "I tried to persuade him that it was Christmas and people didn't work on Christmas Eve, but he only said it depended on the kind of work you did."

"Well, that's true, Robin," said his mother gently, appreciating her younger son's disappointment. "You'll have plenty of time to talk to him tomorrow. I, personally, shall insist he doesn't work on Christmas Day."

"I don't think he looks at all well," declared Nancy, looking up from the sweater coat she was crocheting for her daughter. She subjected Rachel to a cool appraisal. "Are you sure he's looking after himself the way he should?"

Liz chuckled. "I wouldn't mention that to Jaime if I were you, Nancy," she remarked dryly. "Looking after himself is not one of Jaime's virtues."

"In any case, I think he looks okay," declared Robin. "He's as hard as nails, and he wouldn't thank you for your sympathy." He grinned then, and lifted one leg to rest his ankle across his knee. "I'd hazard a guess there's nothing wrong with him that a night with a woman wouldn't put right. What do you say, young Rachel?"

"Robin!"

His wife and his mother both spoke together, and although she was not as scandalized as they were, Rachel herself could have wished he had more discretion. "I wouldn't know anything about that, Robin," she replied composedly, but she could tell from the wicked glint in his eyes that he, for one, didn't believe her. Nevertheless, she had no intention of entering into an argument with him, and when Liz got up to make his sandwich, as Maisie had been given the night off, Rachel offered to help her.

Having left the young couple alone, Rachel would not have been surprised to find them in one another's arms when she returned fifteen minutes later with the tray. Instead she found them in the middle of a heated argument, and as Nancy allotted her a hostile glare when she sat down, she guessed that somehow she had been responsible for the upset.

Going to church soothed her mind at least, and the simple service left her feeling calm and reassured. Back at Clere Heights they were joined by the Armstrongs, who had looked after the baby in their absence, and they all indulged in a Christmas drink and a customary salute under the mistletoe. Fortunately Nancy was a little more mellow by this time, and only Rachel protested when Robin attempted to prolong his privilege.

"Please," she exclaimed, struggling free of him with difficulty, but Robin was seemingly unrepentant.

"Whatever Jaime says, you're more beautiful than ever," he mumbled, half under his breath, "and if he doesn't want you, then what's wrong with me?"

"You're drunk!" said Rachel impatiently, smelling the whiskey on his breath, and then changing her look of tight-lipped irritation to a reluctant smile as Nancy looked their way. "Pull yourself together, for goodness' sake, Robin. Your wife's got her eye on you, and I don't intend to spend the holiday as a bone of contention between you two!"

"Just remember what I said," said Robin, closing one eye deliberately, and Rachel turned away, disgusted, as Nancy came to claim him.

It was a relief to go to bed, to close her door, and know that she had at least seven hours before she need face any of them again. She refused to worry about her door tonight despite what Jaime had said, and although she did not sleep any more soundly than she had done the night before, she did lose consciousness the minute her head touched the pillow.

Yet, in spite of her late night, she was awake early on Christmas morning, almost before it was light, and lay for a while listening to the cock crowing from the farmyard across the field. It was a homely sound, a reassuring sound, and feeling a restlessness that would not let her linger, she decided to take a bath.

It was only a little after eight by the time she was dressed and brushing her hair at the dressing table. In wine-colored corduroy pants and a matching shirt, a maroon velvet vest added for warmth, she gazed at her reflection disconsolately, feeling suddenly isolated on this essentially family festival. She ought not to have come, she thought unhappily, tugging impatiently at an errant strand of chestnut silk. It would have been easier if she had stayed in London, and accepted a friend's invitation instead of coming all this way to stay with people she hardly knew.

She pulled out a tissue and blew her nose, regarding herself critically over the scrap of pink paper. She could hardly blame Jaime for the way she felt, she conceded, although his presence here had thrown her completely off balance. Nevertheless, she was the interloper, not him, whatever Liz and Robert said, and Nancy had every reason to feel aggrieved at her intrusion.

Robin was a nuisance, but she thought she could handle him. It was Jaime who really troubled her; Jaime, who had the ability to make her despise him one minute and herself the next; and if she was feeling lonely now, it was because she was remembering what might have been.

She sighed, cupping her chin on one hand, and gazed blankly into space. She had been so gullible when they met. Looking back now, she could hardly credit the girl she had once been....

SHE HAD STARTED at London Westward Television just before Christmas, one of a number of girls working in a pool of secretaries, called upon by various members of the executive staff. She was happy in her job. It was interesting work. And it meant she could supplement the rather low salary her father received as curator of a small museum in Kensington.

Three months later she met Jaime Shard face to face for the first time.

She was late for work one morning, and just managed to squeeze through the elevator doors as they were closing to find herself sharing the cubicle with one of LWTV's youngest reporters. She recognized him at once, having watched the reports he had brought back from Vietnam on the network's news programs, but he didn't know her from any one of the other secretaries who gazed at him admiringly from a distance. Rachel had already heard him spoken of in tones of envy, and her best friend in the typing pool, Kerry Richards, thought he was the "dishiest" male she had ever seen.

Rachel remembered how breathless she had been after her sprint from the bus stop, and how she had struggled to control her breathing as she pressed the button for her floor. She guessed her hair must be a mess, and the woolen overcoat she was wearing over her navy skirt and blouse had seen better days, and she thought how amused Kerry would be when she relayed her experiences to her.

Jaime, for his part, looked as calm and self-confident as he did on the television screen. He was very tanned, due no doubt to the time he spent in eastern and far-eastern countries, and although his leather vest and jeans were not new, he exuded an aura of sexual sophistication that girls seemed to find irresistible. Not that he cultivated his reputation. On the contrary, in spite of his following, he seemed totally indifferent to the many longing glances cast in his direction, and Kerry had confided that she thought he had a woman tucked away somewhere who satisfied all his masculine needs. Glancing at him now, Rachel decided it was most likely, and knew a moment's impatience at the involuntary quickening of her own pulse.

"I gather you work here."

For a moment Rachel thought she had imagined he was speaking to her, but then, when the statement was repeated, she looked up at him questioningly.

"I—why, yes." Her cool composed features belied the sudden flutter in her stomach. "I work in the typing pool, Mr. Shard. And...I'm late."

He did not remark on her use of his name. It was unlikely that she would not have identified him if she did work here, and instead, he asked, "How long have you worked for LWTV?"

Rachel hesitated. "Almost three months," she replied, wondering why he wanted to know. Then, with relief, she added, "This is my floor."

He inclined his head as she got out, and her legs felt suddenly weak as she walked along the rubber-tiled corridor. It was the first inkling she had that her relationship with Jaime Shard was not going to be easy, and instead of mentioning what had happened to Kerry, she kept it to herself.

She did not see him again for almost six weeks. She heard, through the inevitable grapevine, that he had been sent to one of the small republics in Central America to cover the siege of a university there by a group of students, and later, that he was in Jamaica, covering a conference of heads of state, and she watched his reports with added interest. But when Kerry hinted that she had heard he had been seen dining with a certain American lady reporter in Kingston, Rachel had been dismayed by her own reactions to it. Until then she had regarded Kerry's fervent interest with a certain amount of amusement, and to find herself doing the same, and worse, filled her with disgust.

Consequently, when she was sent for by one of the executives to take some dictation, she was more than a little perturbed to find Jaime in the office, lounging in one of the soft, black leather armchairs, his leg draped lazily over the arm.

"Hello," he said, getting up at her entrance, and she glanced around doubtfully for Mr. Morrison, the producer who had sent for her. She had worked for him several times in the absence of his secretary, who had had appendicitis, but right now only her protagonist faced her across the room.

He was wearing a business suit today, dark and expensive, that fitted his shoulders and the muscled length of his legs with loving closeness. The white collar of his shirt accentuated the deeper tan he had acquired, and his dark hair was combed smoothly to lie thickly against his head. He looked sleek and handsome, like a well-groomed male animal, and Rachel was aware of him with every fiber of her being.

"Jack won't be long," he remarked now, indicating the chair at the opposite side of the desk. "Sit down. There's no charge."

Rachel moved slowly across the room and sat down stiffly, crossing her legs. Then, realizing he might think she was trying to draw his attention to their slender shapeliness, she uncrossed them again, pressing her knees together, and gripping the pad tightly in her lap.

Jaime studied her evident constraint for several minutes, and then, surprising her, came around the desk to prop himself on its edge beside her. "Is something wrong?" he inquired with gentle irony. "You're not afraid of Jack, are you? He's a nice guy. Believe me!"

"I'm not afraid of anyone," Rachel retorted aloofly, wishing he would go back around the desk. "I know Mr. Morrison. I've worked for him before. I . . . I just didn't expect to find you here, Mr. Shard. Mr. Morrison isn't connected with current affairs, is he?"

"Oh, I see." Jaime's mouth compressed in comprehension. "It's me you don't like, not Jack. I'm sorry." He grimaced. "What did I do to earn your disapproval?"

Rachel sighed. "I think you're making fun of me, Mr. Shard," she said at length, determined not to let him see how he had disconcerted her, and he straightened away from the desk to regard her curiously.

"What's your name?" he asked, disrupting her still further, and she looked up at him apprehensively, wondering if he intended to report her for insolence.

"Williams," she answered in a low voice. "Rachel Williams," and then looked down at her hands in her lap, feeling like a disobedient schoolgirl.

"Well, Rachel Williams, as it happens, Jack Morrison is an old friend of mine," said Jaime flatly. "That's why I'm here, waiting for him. Does that answer your question?"

"I...I didn't—"

"Ask the question? No. But you implied the inquiry."

Rachel moved her shoulders helplessly. "I...shouldn't have. I'm sorry."

"That's all right." With a likewise shrug, Jaime left her, walking around the desk to take up his previous position, regarding her across the array of metal trays and telephones, and scattered files and papers with narrow-eyed appraisal.

When Mr. Morrison appeared, he greeted Jaime warmly, and they both disappeared outside the office again to exchange a few words in private. Rachel breathed more freely now that she no longer felt herself being scrutinized, but although she told herself she was glad he had gone, she couldn't help wishing she had been less reticent and taken advantage of her opportunities. Not that she imagined a man like him might be interested in a girl of eighteen, but she had probably given him the impression that she was sullen and totally lacking in personality, not a good opinion for anyone to have of her.

Once again she forbore to tell Kerry about the encounter, unwilling to involve herself in a detailed résumé of what had happened. Somehow she was loath to discuss Jaime Shard with anyone, and although she felt a bit mean, she couldn't help it.

The weather was getting warmer, and Rachel took to walking home some evenings, enjoying the sunlit saunter across the park. Her father was never home before seven-thirty, after the museum had closed, so she had plenty of time to walk the distance and still have a meal prepared for him.

One evening, after working later than usual, she decided she had better take the bus, and was propped against the post, flicking over the pages of a magazine, when a sleek green sports car pulled alongside her.

She stepped back instinctively, used to parrying the proffered lifts of strangers who were attracted by the sight of a girl alone, and then felt her lips part in astonishment when the driver leaned across the passenger seat to push open the door.

"Can I give you a lift?" Jaime Shard's mouth twisted in wry self-derision. "It's hackneyed, I know, but it's the best I can do."

"But... why?" Rachel gazed down at him helplessly, and he moved his shoulders in an offhand gesture.

"Because I saw you. Because I feel like it. Because you're a very attractive girl, and you... interest me."

Rachel caught her breath. "But I can't. I mean... you don't live near where I do."

Jaime sighed. "Is that a refusal?" He glanced around. "Because I'm on double yellow lines, and I'd prefer not to have to pay another fine."

Rachel looped her bag over her shoulder and rolled the hapless magazine between her fingers. She ought to refuse, she knew that, and had it been anyone else she would have done so without hesitation. But, although she had always considered herself capable of controlling every situation, Jaime Shard disturbed her as none of the young men she had dated had done. And it wasn't as if he was dating her, after all. He was offering her a lift, nothing more. But if, as he had stated, she interested him, what else might the lift entail?

"Make up your mind," he exclaimed impatiently, and she cast caution to the wind.

"Thank you," she said, and climbed into the low bucket seat, and he pressed hard on the accelerator as the bus appeared behind them.

"I am not in the habit of doing this sort of thing," she admitted stiffly, after he had asked her address, and he gave her a hard sidelong glance.

"Believe it or not, nor am I," he retorted curtly, and she realized she had annoyed him by hesitating so long.

"Have...have you been away again?" she ventured, as they turned into Kensington Road, realizing it was several weeks since she had seen him in Mr. Morrison's office, and after a few moments Jaime nodded.

"I've been on holiday," he conceded without expression. "You did say Latimer Square, didn't you?"

"That's right." Rachel cast a doubtful smile in his direction. "This...this is very kind of you, you know. I...I was late leaving the office tonight."

"I know." Jaime made no attempt to elucidate on this statement, and Rachel felt a helpless sense of bewilderment. How did he know these things about her? Had it just been chance that brought him along at this particular time of day? And if not, why had he chosen her to be the object of his attentions?

In no time at all it seemed, they were pulling up outside her home, a small terraced house in a quiet street in North Kensington. She had never been more conscious of its Victorian inelegance or the shabby state of its paint, but apparently such considerations did not occur to Jaime.

"You live with your father, don't you?" he remarked, glancing up at the lace-curtained windows that looked old-fashioned among so many modernized exteriors. "Your mother's dead, and you've got no brothers or sisters, am I right? And your father's the curator at Harlings."

Rachel, who had been about to get out, turned to stare at him with incredulous eyes. "How do you know?"

"You forget—it's my job to get information," he retorted. And then, with less forcefulness, he said, "I told you—I was interested."

"But why?" Rachel gazed at him, and his lean mouth twisted.

"Why not?"

"But... you don't know me."

"Does it bother you? I'll confess—I looked up your record."

Rachel shook her head. "Why me?"

"Aren't you flattered?"

"Not much." She made a helpless gesture. "I don't understand, Mr. Shard."

He half turned in his seat toward her, drawing his knee up onto the seat, laying his arm along the back of hers. It was a warm evening, and he had shed his jacket, so that the lean tanned length of his arm was behind her, bare below the sleeve of his sweat shirt. It was only a couple of inches from her neck, and she was very aware of it, just as she was aware of him, of his masculine scent, and the covering of fine body hair that disappeared below the opened neck of his shirt.

"Perhaps that's why," he said now, surveying her through narrowed eyes. "Because you're... shy."

"Naive, you mean."

"No. I don't mean naive."

Rachel flushed. "You're making fun of me again."

"I've never made fun of you," he retorted crisply.

"Amusing yourself, then."

"No."

Rachel drew a deep breath. "I suppose you know, half the girls at LWTV think—well, they'd be very flattered."

"But not you."

Rachel faltered. "Why did you pick me up? It wasn't to make a date."

"Wasn't it?" His eyes narrowed. "Why not?"

She sighed. "You don't make dates. At least...not with the girls at the station."

Jaime's eyes grew mocking. "How would you know that?"

Rachel bent her head, the heavy weight of her hair slipping forward, exposing the vulnerable curve of her nape. "I have to go, Mr. Shard. My father will be home soon, and I have dinner to prepare."

"Have dinner with me," he offered carelessly, his brown eyes probingly intent. "After you've prepared your father's dinner, of course."

Rachel looped the right side of her hair behind her ear and peered at him. "I...I don't think so."

"Don't you want to?"

Did she want to? Rachel remembered the struggle she had had to disguise how much. But she was very much afraid he was out of her league, and she suspected he would want more from her than just a simple good-night kiss afterward.

"If you're afraid I'm planning to rape you, forget it," he told her then, his tone hard and cynical. "I don't go for that scene. Sex with a prudish little virgin isn't really my line."

"Then why are you asking me?" she demanded, her face flushed from his insult, and he swung around abruptly behind the wheel.

"God knows!" he declared, starting the engine. "Perhaps I'm a masochist! Go on. Get out. I'm late for an appointment as it is."

Rachel groped for the door handle, feeling utterly wretched. She had handled the whole affair so badly, and to add to her humiliation, she knew she was denying something fundamental to her happiness.

Biting her lips, she hesitated, her eyes on his hard, set face. Then, she said doubtfully, "Is...is the invitation still on?"

Jaime swore, and turned his head frustratedly. "Are you kidding?"

"Is it?"

"Damn you, I don't know."

"Because, if it is...I accept." She got out breathily, struggling onto the pavement. "What...what time will you come back?"

RACHEL GOT UP from the dressing table and walked across to the window. That had been the start, of course. And she *had* been naive, she thought impatiently. She had believed what she wanted to believe, and shut her ears to anyone's advice but her own.

Her father's voice had initially been the loudest, telling

her she was a fool to get involved with a man like him, assuring her that no good could come from it, that a serious commitment was not what Jaime had in mind.

He had been right, of course, and in the beginning she had argued that she liked it that way. She and Jaime were good friends, that was all. He took her to dinner, and to the theater, and occasionally to parties, when he was in London, and when he was away, she felt free to make dates with other men.

It was a good relationship in those early months, and Kerry and the other girls in the office held her in some awe for having succeeded in dating the elusive Mr. Shard. They were jealous, of course, and occasionally someone would make some malicious remark about what Jaime did while he was away and with whom he spent his time on those nights Rachel didn't see him. But generally she told herself she was happy with the way things were, and gradually her father's protests died down.

She supposed it was about a year after they first started dating that the situation between them changed dramatically.

Her father had a mild heart attack and was taken into hospital for a few day's observation. Rachel discovered that one of the doctors who was treating her father was the brother of a boy she had gone to school with, and when he offered to drive her home after visiting her father, she invited him in for a cup of coffee.

Jaime was away on an assignment in Japan, and she knew he wasn't expected back for another three days, and she was astonished when the doorbell rang while she and Dr. Fowles were drinking their coffee.

It was Jaime, unshaven and haggard-eyed, after the long flight from Tokyo, and after bestowing the usual almost-brotherly kiss on her cheek, he told her he had come straight from the airport.

"It was a bloody lousy trip, and I wanted to see you," he said simply, and then stiffened abruptly as they entered the living room and found Roderick Fowles getting up from his chair.

What happened next Rachel chose to skim over, recalling Jaime's insolence with a shiver of revulsion. He had been so rude, so totally lacking in the courtesy and respect she had grown used to expecting from him, and poor Roderick had made his escape as quickly as he decently could.

When they were alone she had turned on Jaime with a furious sense of outrage. He was not her keeper, she told him. He knew she dated other men. And he had no right to behave as if he had exclusive rights to her company.

"My father's ill. Rod is one of the doctors looking after him. What do you imagine daddy will think if Rod tells him how he was treated?"

"I don't give a damn what your father thinks," Jaime muttered ungraciously, loosening his tie and unfastening the top two buttons of his shirt. "I would imagine he'd react as I did, finding you entertaining a stranger alone in the house."

"I'm not a child, Jaime!" Rachel retorted stiffly. "And if I choose to invite friends—men friends—into my home, I don't have to get anyone's permission!"

Jaime glared down at her angrily, his jaw working, as if he was endeavoring to control some violent emotion. "I don't want you inviting any men to your home," he stated grimly. "I don't even want you dating any other men! Dammit, I've tried to play the game the way you want it, but it's tearing me to pieces."

Rachel moved her head disbelievingly. "Jaime?" she breathed, putting out a hand toward him, and then felt herself caught and jerked close against him. For the first time she felt the burning heat of his mouth covering hers, and her head swam beneath the hungry passion of his kiss.

Until that moment her experiences with men had all been innocent. The nearest she had ever come to sex was in allowing a boy during her secretarial-college days to stroke her breasts, and that only through the layers of her clothing. She had not liked it. She had resented his proprietorial touch on her body, and since then, none of the young men she had dated had been allowed such liberties.

With Jaime it was different. It was as if she had been waiting for him to hold her, to touch her, to treat her body as his own possession. She had been wearing a shirt, she remembered, fastened through to the waist, and Jaime had disposed of the buttons urgently, and exposed her rounded breasts to his view. Those hard brown hands had caressed her jealously, while his tongue played havoc with her senses. Whatever kind of life he had led, he was certainly knowledgeable of the way to arouse her, and her knees buckled weakly as he sought her mouth again.

"I think you'd better go make some more coffee," he muttered at last, pushing her away from him, and she drew back half in protest, drawing the sides of her shirt around her. Jaime shed his jacket onto the couch, and raked unsteady fingers through his hair. He turned away to pick up his briefcase, evidently trying to get himself in control, and for what happened afterward, Rachel could only blame herself.

He straightened after dropping the briefcase beside his jacket, putting his hands into his pockets as if searching for his key. As he did so, Rachel crossed the space between them, sliding her arms around his waist from behind.

"Thank you," she said, pressing herself against the hard expanse of his back, and felt the convulsive shudder that went through him.

"Rachel," he said, and his voice was harsh with warning now. "Rachel, don't do this. Don't play with fire!"

"And if I want to?" she breathed, allowing her hands to slide down over his flat stomach to his thighs. "Why shouldn't I touch you? You wanted to touch me."

"Rachel, for God's sake!" He caught her hands, and stilled their sensuous exploration, expelling his breath on a gulp. "Rachel, we're alone here, and this is madness. Don't do something you're going to regret."

"Why should I regret it?" she demanded, her voice half-resentful. "Why shouldn't I do as you do? I bet your other girls do."

"What other girls?" he grated savagely, twisting around to face her. "There are no other . . . girls! And you—you're different."

"A virgin, you mean?" she choked. "Of course you don't like virgins. You told me that once. I'd forgotten."

"Don't be so bloody stupid!" he snapped, taking her by the shoulders and shaking her angrily. "I said you could trust me, and I haven't done anything to betray that. But God knows, I'm only human and I do want you!"

Rachel's lips quivered. "Oh, Jaime," she breathed, tugging his shirt apart, and pressing herself against the fine dark hair on his chest. "I'm so glad you came home so unexpectedly. I thought I just didn't turn you on...."

Of course he did not return to his apartment that night, nor in fact for any of the nights that her father spent in hospital. Indeed, it was difficult to get him out of bed in the mornings, and being late for work became almost a daily hazard.

Looking back on it now, Rachel knew she had never been happier than when she and Jaime were together. They were good together, both in bed and out of it, and when her father returned from hospital she began to spend nights at Jaime's apartment.

Eventually one of their neighbors thought it her duty to tell Rachel's father that a green Ferrari had been parked outside his door during the nights while he was in hospital. She had just thought Mr. Williams ought to know what was going on, she said, and Rachel's father had thanked her, before confronting his daughter with the gossip.

"I thought you said you were only good friends," he accused her tautly. "Rachel, don't let him use you like this. It's for your own good I'm telling you."

Naturally Rachel didn't believe him. She was too much in love with Jaime to listen to any criticism of him, and the weeks when he was out of the country dragged by. When he first took her north to meet his parents, she had been in seventh heaven, convinced he intended to marry her, and even indifferent to the implications of overhearing another woman's name mentioned in protest by his mother. It was the first time she heard of Betsy, and her stomach contracted now in memory of what that name came to mean to her.

Her father was taken ill again, and spent three months in a nursing home. Jaime was sweet to her, taking her to visit him every day, arranging for her father to have a private room and color television, and anything else he required. Mr. Williams had protested that he didn't want anything from a man like Jaime Shard, but Rachel knew that he secretly enjoyed his privileges, and began to look forward to the games of chess that Jaime instigated.

When her father was well enough to come home, Jaime arranged for him to have a private nurse, and then took Rachel to Northumberland again. He said she needed the break, and she did. The worry over her father had drained her, but during the two weeks in August they spent with his family, she grew relaxed and strong again, blossoming daily in her love for Jaime. They were never apart. They could never get enough of one another. And if his parents suspected that Rachel did not sleep in her own room, they kept their opinions to themselves.

Of course, eventually, they had to go back, and almost immediately Jaime was sent abroad. He had succeeded in avoiding all overseas assignments during the summer, but now his work caught up with him, and Rachel had to content herself with taking care of her father.

Then, one afternoon in early October, Betsy came to see her.

She said she was Jaime's wife, that she had been his wife for five years, and that she had come to Rachel in a last attempt to save her marriage.

Rachel was shaken, appalled, incredulous and, finally, bitterly humiliated. No one, but no one, had ever mentioned that Jaime had been—or *was*—married. It had never been mentioned. Of course she had heard the usual gossip, particularly the story that he was keeping a woman somewhere, but she had stopped believing it when she and Jaime became lovers. She would never have believed he had anyone else, would never have thought him capable of such duplicity. But now this woman, Betsy, was telling her that he owned a house in Buckinghamshire, near Aylesbury, in fact, and that he still lived with her there, when he could find the time.

All those occasions when he had supposedly been out of the country, poured back into Rachel's mind like a flood. How did she really know he had been out of the country as long as he said? He could easily have come back a few days earlier, as he had done from Japan, she remembered chillingly, and she felt physically sick as she faced his wife.

But there was worse to come. She was pregnant, Betsy said. With their first child. She had wanted a baby for so long, and now that it had happened, she had discovered he had another woman. *Another woman! Herself!* Rachel blanched. No wonder he had never spoken of marriage...to her!

She didn't know how she got through that meeting, or indeed, remember much of what Betsy looked like. She was petite, she thought, blond, and rather delicate-looking, with limpid blue eyes, and rather wet lips, which she continually moistened. The things that really stuck in Rachel's mind were the wedding ring on Betsy's finger and the legality of her marriage certificate.

After she was gone, so many things fell into place in Rachel's mind, not least of all Betsy's name, which she had heard mentioned in an undertone at Clere Heights.

When Jaime arrived back from the Middle East, she at first refused to see him, but then, realizing she could conceivably be doing him some terrible injustice, she agreed to speak with him.

She knew at once that he knew about Betsy's visit, and that seemed to settle everything. The very fact that he was still seeing his wife said it all, and she refused to listen when he tried to tell her that they were separated, and had been for the last three years. He did not deny that his wife lived in Buckinghamshire, he did not deny that he had never sued for a divorce, and although he denied all knowledge of it, the fact remained that Betsy was pregnant.

It was the end. They both knew it. Rachel resigned from her job at LWTV and took another with a rival station, while Jaime was forced to go on with his commitments. He tried to phone her several times, and when that didn't work, he wrote her letters. Although she wanted to send them back unopened, curiosity got the better of her, and through them she learned that Betsy had had a miscarriage. But she never replied, though she did keep in touch with his parents, and forgave them for their part in the deception.

Curiously enough, her father took their breakup badly. After all the things he had said about Jaime in the past, he defended him when Rachel reviled him for his deceit. Things were not always what they seemed, he said, advising her not to be hasty, but the facts were there, and Rachel could not look beyond them.

She ran an unsteady hand over her hair now, gazing out over the frost-rimmed lawns with unseeing eyes. She wondered where Betsy was now, what she was doing. Did she still live in the house near Aylesbury? Was she still his legal wife? And did Jaime ever stay there, as he used to in the past?

CHAPTER FIVE

HER PALMS WERE MOIST as she turned away from the window, and needing to escape from the increasing desperation of her thoughts, she opened her door. The corridor outside was quiet. The family was still sleeping, she guessed, and closing her door behind her, she went softly down the stairs.

The house was still quite chilly. The central heating system had not yet gained its full strength, and she hunched her shoulders against the cold as she opened the library door. Like the sitting room, there was usually an open fire in the library, and if Maisie was already around, which seemed likely, she had probably lighted it by now.

She stopped short at the sight that confronted her. Jaime was stretched out, asleep, on the leather sofa to one side of the empty grate, an open book spread-eagle on the rug beside him. She guessed he had been reading when he fell asleep, and as she automatically bent to pick it up, she saw the empty bottle of Scotch that had rolled beneath the sofa.

Straightening, she looked down at him tensely, trying to dispel the unwilling sense of responsibility she was experiencing. Had his leg been hurting him? Was that why he had come downstairs to find a book? And why had he needed the whiskey? She had never known him to get drunk before. But then, she acknowledged bitterly, there were a lot of things she had not known about him, so why should one more surprise be of any consequence to her?

He was still fully dressed in the dark green velvet pants and vest he had worn over the white silk shirt for dinner. There was no sign of his jacket, which he had apparently shed upstairs, and his tie, too, had been abandoned to facilitate the unfastening of his shirt. With his dark hair disordered and untidy, and his lean, intelligent features softened in sleep, he seemed curiously defenseless, and Rachel steeled her heart. It was too soon after her recollection of what they had been to one another for her to view him objectively, and his reclining indolence reminded her vividly of the mornings she had awakened to find him beside her. She remembered him awakening her with kisses, making love before it was hardly light, and then sleeping until midmorning, when he would drag himself up and out to the studios. She could not imagine herself ever having that kind of relationship with anybody else, and even knowing him for the devil he was, she perceived the ache inside her, and knew what it presaged.

"Merry Christmas!"

She was unaware his eyes had opened, and when he spoke to her, she started, folding her arms around the book and holding it half protectively to her chest.

"M-merry Christmas," she responded, moving her shoulders awkwardly. "I—why—you're up early this morning."

His expression conveyed that he knew that she was skating around the truth and, grimacing, he sat up and swung his stiffened legs to the floor. "God! It's cold!" he muttered, as an involuntary shudder passed over him. "Is Maisie around yet? I could sure use a cup of tea."

Rachel glanced over her shoulder. "I'll go and see, if you like." Then she added reluctantly, "You should have used a blanket. It's crazy to fall asleep uncovered at this time of year. You could catch your death of cold!"

"I thought I was just supposed to have got up," Jaime remarked laconically, and she shifted uncomfortably. And as if satisfied that he had disconcerted her, he added, "I was reinforced with a drop of the hard stuff." He frowned. "I guess I must have dropped off."

"Passed out, more likely," retorted Rachel vehemently. "There's an empty bottle of Scotch beneath the sofa. I doubt there was just a 'drop' in it when you sat down."

"We have been a busy little bee, haven't we?" Jaime regarded her beneath lowered lids. "What business is it of yours if I choose to indulge my weaknesses? This is my home...and my Scotch!"

Rachel flushed. "It's no business of mine, of course," she admitted stiffly, unfolding her arms from around the book and setting it down carefully on the edge of the bookshelf beside her. She hesitated. "I, er, I'll go and see about some tea. I think I can hear—"

"No, wait!" With a stifled oath, Jaime struggled up from the sofa, and dragged himself with difficulty toward her. "What I said about this being my home wasn't meant to sound the way it did. You know you're as welcome here as I am, anytime."

"Thank you. You don't have to explain yourself to me,"

she responded tautly, holding herself rigidly in front of him. "I know how welcome your parents have made me. And I appreciate it. But it is your home, you're correct, and I had no right to pass any criticism—"

"Rachel, I'm tired, that's all," he muttered roughly. "And I guess I don't always choose the right words." He shook his head. "I drank because I couldn't sleep, does that excuse me?" He clenched his fists. "Just tell me, how the hell was I supposed to sleep after what happened yesterday afternoon?"

Rachel moved automatically toward the door. She didn't trust him in this mood, and of a certainty, she didn't trust herself. With a muffled word of explanation, she went to find Maisie, and glimpsed over her shoulder the weary way he hunched his shoulders as he flung himself back onto the sofa.

Breakfast was a family meal, when all the presents were exchanged. Rachel, who had had no foreknowledge of Jaime's presence, had only been able to buy him a box containing shaving soap and after-shave lotion at the village shop the previous day, but she had a scarf for Robert, some French perfume for Liz, chocolates for Robin and Nancy, and a cuddly toy for the baby.

She was surprised and touched by the present the Shards gave her. It was an oval cameo brooch, obviously very old, but in beautiful condition, with the words, "To Amy, with love," engraved on the back.

"It's been in my family for generations," Liz confided after Rachel had given them both a rather emotional embrace. "It belonged to my great-grandmother originally, and it's been passed down from mother to daughter for the last hundred years or so." She smiled. "And as I don't have a daughter to give it to, I thought you might like to have it."

Rachel was overwhelmed, but she glanced rather doubtfully at Nancy, and Liz intercepted her uncertainty.

"We've given Nancy grandmother's pearls," she said, understanding perfectly how Rachel must be feeling. "But I wanted you to have the brooch. I was sure you'd appreciate it."

"Oh, I do," Rachel found Jaime's eyes upon her, but couldn't meet their intense appraisal. Indeed, she had not seen him since his impassioned denunciation in the library. She had asked Maisie to take him his tea while she peeled mushrooms in the kitchen, and if the housekeeper found it strange that their guest preferred such a menial task to serving her employer's eldest son, she kept her opinion to herself.

But now Rachel could not avoid his attention, and she was relieved when Liz exclaimed at the present Jaime had brought her, and passed the delicate gold wristwatch around the table for everyone to see.

Robin and Nancy gave Rachel some handkerchiefs, and she thanked them warmly before turning to the final package beside her plate. She knew from the handwriting on the card that accompanied it that this was from Jaime, and she fumbled with the fastening, apprehensive of what it might be. He had given his father and his brother cufflinks, and Nancy a silver bracelet, and she couldn't imagine what he could have bought her when he hadn't even known she would be here until five days ago.

It was a ring. After the wrapping paper had fallen aside to reveal an incongruously large box, Rachel suspected it might be an ornament of some sort, possibly a souvenir from his unfortunate trip to Masota, but she was wrong. When the cardboard lid was removed and the tissue paper proved to be only packing, she eventually discovered her quarry at the bottom of the box, wrapped simply in a scrap of blue velvet.

The ring was made of gold, with a ruby at its heart, and a handful of small diamonds to serve as its mounting. It was evidently valuable, and judging by the looks his family were exchanging, as much of a surprise to them as it had been to her, and Rachel felt hopelessly embarrassed.

"Do you like it?"

It was Jaime who posed the question, and she looked at him reluctantly, striving for inspiration. "I—it's very nice," she murmured, "but...but I can't take it," she added quickly. "I never thought—I mean, I never expected anything like this, and...and honestly, I don't know what to say."

"Try it on," advised Jaime flatly, pouring himself more coffee. "At least give me the satisfaction of seeing if it fits you."

Rachel glanced doubtfully at his mother, but Liz nodded. "Yes. Try it on, Rachel," she urged, ignoring Nancy's disapproving expression, and with a helpless shrug of her shoulders, Rachel complied.

It was a tiny bit tight. The fingers of her right hand were infinitesimally bigger than her left, but although the implication was obvious, Rachel refused to acknowledge it. She had no idea how or why Jaime would have bought her such an expensive present, and no matter how much she liked it, she could not keep it.

"Oh, darling, it looks lovely!" Liz hadn't an atom of envy in her body, and she stretched out her hand across the table to tilt Rachel's fingers toward her. "Rob, isn't it beautiful?" Then she said to her son, "I bet you didn't get this in England!"

"It's from Tiffanys, actually," remarked Jaime, throwing away the name of the famous New York jeweler without a second thought.

"Tiffanys!" exclaimed Nancy enviously. "Robin, why don't you ever buy me anything like that?"

Rachel tugged off the ring again as Robin made some good-natured complaint about overpaid journalists, and wrapped it back up in the blue velvet. "It . . . it was very kind of you, Jaime," she murmured, speaking with difficulty, "but really, it's not anything I could accept."

"Why not?"

His brown eyes had darkened, putting her on the spot, and she realized he had given it to her in front of the others deliberately. "Because, well, because it's too . . . expensive," she demurred uneasily. "You . . . you shouldn't have spent your money on me."

"I didn't!"

His response was careless, and Rachel glanced awkwardly around at the faces of his family. "What . . . what do you mean?" she ventured. "You must have. Unless—" she forced a tight smile "—unless you stole it."

Jaime looked at her over the rim of his coffee cup, and

she could not read his expression. "It's like the brooch," he said at last, putting his cup back on its saucer. And as she arched her brows in some confusion, he added, "It's not new. I've had it for...some time." He paused. "I forget why I bought it now."

"Even so—" Rachel pushed the box toward him, but he propelled it back.

"Keep it," he said. "It's of no use to me. It fits you. Wear it...with my...blessing."

Rachel's face was burning, and realizing she could not go on arguing with him in front of his parents, she allowed the box to remain beside her plate. But her eyes still battled with his arrogance, until the mocking gleam in his defeated her.

After the breakfast dishes were cleared away, and baby Lisa had been fed, Liz suggested that the young people go for a walk. "Jaime can't, of course," she said, looking at her elder son, who was still sitting at the table, "but you could go with them, Rob, while I help Maisie."

Robert agreed, and the four of them set off with the baby, safely ensconced in her pram, accompanying them. They took the cliff path this time, following the track that led around the curve of the headland, and trekked across an area of wild gorse and scrubland that eventually gave onto a sandy cove. It was a way Rachel had once known intimately, having walked this way with Jaime many times in the past, and it took a deal of willpower to keep those thoughts at bay, with the incident of the ring still uppermost in her thoughts.

Robert had charge of the pram, and as he started to ask

Robin some questions regarding the steel works, Rachel found herself walking behind with Nancy. The path was only wide enough for two to walk abreast, so the two girls fell into step together, neither of them being given much choice.

It was a cold frosty morning, but the sky was high and clear, and the sun made little impression. It was invigorating to walk with its warmth on their backs, and the shifting waters of the North Sea beside them, and deciding it was up to her, Rachel tried to be friendly.

"Lisa's quite big for two months, isn't she?" she tendered, not really knowing much about babies, but impressed even so by the baby's energy. "I expect she'll be quite a handful when she gets older. Do you think she takes after Robin?"

Nancy shrugged, pushing her hands deeper into the pockets of the dark fur coat she was wearing. With her blond hair, it was quite a contrast, and Rachel guessed she considered her appearance quite striking.

"I don't know what Robin was like as a baby," Nancy retorted at last, when Rachel had begun to think she wasn't going to answer her. "We've only been married for fifteen months. I didn't even want to have a baby!"

"Didn't you?" Rachel tried to be sympathetic. "You mean...straight away, I suppose."

"No. I'm not the maternal type!" Nancy was scornful. "But, men are so beastly selfish, and before I knew where I was, she was on the way."

"I see." Rachel absorbed this thoughtfully. "Well, never mind, I'm sure you'll know better next time."

"Yes." Nancy hunched her shoulders. "Only it's such a

rotten business. I think men should take care of that sort of thing, don't you?"

Rachel controlled her color with difficulty and made a dismissing gesture. "I suppose it depends on the individual," she said carefully. "I believe you can get advice on the subject."

"Advice!" Nancy was contemptuous. "Oh, I've had advice, all right. But who wants to take their ghastly drugs? I don't. They make me feel so sick."

Rachel bit her lip. "Well, I think you ought to take more advice," she said seriously. "They are various drugs on the market. What you've been taking obviously isn't your type. I would try again."

Nancy eyed her maliciously. "You seem to know a lot about it." She narrowed her eyes. "Did you and Jaime—"

Rachel squared her shoulders. "I'd really rather not discuss it," she declared firmly. "Is that an oil tanker out there, do you think?"

Nancy didn't take the hint. "Robin says you and his brother used to be really close," she persisted slyly. "I don't blame you, you know. He's really attractive, isn't he? Sort of . . . sexy, but clever with it."

"Really, Nancy, I don't think—"

"Oh, don't get on your high horse with me, Rachel. Robin's told me all about you. How you and Jaime went around together for almost three years. How he brought you up here to meet his parents. You can't tell me you kept his interest for that long without getting into bed with him! I just won't believe you." She laughed rather enviously. "And who'd want to stop him?"

"Nancy!" Rachel was astounded, but the younger girl only pulled a face.

"Well! At least you kept your figure! Have you any idea how awful it is to swell up like a big balloon!"

Rachel had to smile. In some ways Nancy was still very naive. And besides, she acknowledged with a pang, there was a time when she had been tempted to let herself get pregnant. She had wanted Jaime's baby so much. But common sense, and her father's frailty, had prevailed, and afterward it was too late....

"That's a beautiful ring he gave you, isn't it?" Nancy continued now as they began the descent to the cove. "It must have cost a lot of money." She hesitated. "Are you two back together again?"

"No!" Rachel spoke vehemently, glad that the color in her face could be attributed to the wind, and was unutterably relieved when Robert turned and urged them to catch up with him and Robin.

Lunch was ready by the time they got back, a cold buffet-type meal served in the morning room. Christmas dinner would be served that evening, after the Shards' other guests had arrived, and Liz explained to Rachel that there would be fourteen altogether.

"You haven't met Rob's director, Bernard Hylton, have you?" she asked as Rachel was helping her to set the dining-room table, specially extended for the occasion. "I think you'll like the Hyltons. They're a nice couple. And their daughter, Angela, must be about your age."

"Is she coming with them?" Rachel inquired, sorting knives and forks, and Liz nodded.

"They have a son, too, but he won't be joining us. He got

married a few months ago, and he and his wife are spending Christmas with her parents.''

"Well, that's nine," said Rachel, counting the six of them, and the three Hyltons. "Who else would I know?"

Liz stopped what she was doing to consider. "You know Mr. Conway, the vicar, of course. He and his wife will be joining us. And the Mannings." She mentioned the name of the local doctor. "Oh, and their son, Patrick. Just to even the numbers."

Rachel inclined her head. "What time are they likely to arrive?"

Liz began folding napkins. "Well, the Mannings and Mr. Conway won't be here until after seven, but I would think Bernard and Alice will be here in time for tea."

"That's ... Mr. and Mrs. Hylton?" Rachel was trying to remember names.

"And Angela," agreed Liz, smiling, and patted the girl's arm affectionately as she went toward the door. "You're being a big help, darling, and I'm grateful. What with the baby and everything, Nancy doesn't have the time to help out. But I know I can rely on you."

Rachel returned her smile. "It's the least I can do," she replied, really meaning it. "I could have spent Christmas alone."

Liz hesitated. "So ... you and Jaime; it's not been as bad as you expected?"

Rachel bent her head. "We're civil to one another."

"I noticed that." Liz paused. "But I also noticed that you left his gift on the table in the morning room. I put it in your room before lunch."

"Oh, Liz—"

"At least leave it there for the time being," Liz appealed urgently. "I'd rather not leave a valuable ring like that lying around, and I know Jaime won't take it back."

Rachel sighed, but Jaime's mother looked so anxious she could not disappoint her. "All right," she said without rancor, and Liz squeezed her shoulders before hurrying away.

The table was finished, and Rachel admired their handiwork before leaving the room. The centerpiece of holly and mistletoe and white Christmas roses, was flanked by tall red candles in silver candlesticks, just waiting to be lighted. There were red napkins, vivid on white damask, silver cutlery, polished and gleaming, and long-stemmed crystal glasses, cut to diffuse the light. When the food was served and the wine was poured, it could not look any better than it did at present, she thought with some satisfaction, and decided there were pleasures to be found in simple things that she had hardly apprehended.

She could hear the sound of men's voices coming from the library as she crossed the hall toward the stairs, and assumed Robert and his sons were sharing a lazy afternoon by the fire. Nancy had taken the baby upstairs after lunch, ostensibly to put Lisa down for a nap, but she hadn't reappeared again, and Rachel guessed she was preparing for the dinner party. The Armstrongs had offered to babysit again, and were going to take Lisa to their apartment, which was attached to the main building but entirely independent of it, and no doubt Nancy wanted to make the most of her unexpected freedom.

In her own room Rachel found the box containing Jaime's present sitting on the dressing table. Mrs. Shard had discarded the wrapping paper, and only the box and its velvet-wrapped contents remained, a disturbing reminder that he was still a source of danger to her.

Unwrapped, the ring gleamed dully in the fading light of the winter's afternoon. But nothing could hide its beauty, and on impulse, Rachel slipped it onto her engagement finger.

It fitted perfectly and she held out her hand, spreading her fingers to admire it more fully. How had he acquired such a ring, she asked herself frustratedly. Why should he have such a ring in his possession? Unless—and as the thought occurred to her, she pulled off the ring abruptly—unless it had belonged to Betsy, and she had given it back.

With a sense of revulsion, she wrapped the ring up again and thrust it into the box. Now that the idea had implanted itself in her head, she could not get rid of it, and even the sight of the box that contained it was offensive to her. She didn't want to have to look at it. She didn't want to be reminded where it had come from, and after a moment's hesitation, she got to her feet and picked up the box.

The corridor outside her room was deserted, and after checking that no one was about, she walked swiftly to Jaime's door. She would put the box in his room. He would never know who had put it there. And if he suspected it was his mother, he might have second thoughts before returning it to Rachel again.

Without hesitation she opened the door, and slipped inside. It took only a moment to cross the brown-and-gold patterned carpet, and place the box on the table beside his bed, but after it was done, she did not immediately make her escape. Something, some reluctant sense of nostalgia, caused her to linger a moment, to look around the room that had once been so familiar to her, to absorb with bitter-sweet poignancy, the appointments she remembered.

Jaime's bed, like hers, was a square four-poster, with a mattress overlaid by a gold brocade spread, but the bed, like the room, was bigger and faced east across the gray expanse of the ocean. Rachel moved now, sliding her fingers over the heavy chest of drawers that stood beside the double wardrobe, stroking the backs of the tortoiseshell brushes that resided on the dressing table, and paused in the window embrasure to stare out at the darkening sea.

In her absorption in her surroundings, she had not noticed the line of light beneath the bathroom door, and when it was suddenly opened, and a shaft of brilliance thrown across the carpet, she turned with a gasp, a hand to her mouth, to find Jaime standing there looking at her.

CHAPTER SIX

RACHEL'S INITIAL SENSE OF HUMILIATION in being caught in
such an ignominious position was not helped by the fact
that Jaime's only attire was a pair of brief cotton trunks.
Above them, the brown expanse of his chest and shoulders
was bare, with the light covering of fine dark hair arrowing
down to his navel, and disappearing beneath the waistband
of the black trunks. He was apparently in the process of
changing the dressing on his leg, and Rachel's blood quickened at the sight of the raw, ugly wound in his thigh. Her
eyes were drawn to it automatically, to the ruthlessly torn
muscle and the purplish flesh around it, and then Jaime
spoke and she tilted her head, hiding her involuntary reaction.

"What do you want?" he demanded, coming into the
room with evident difficulty, dragging his injured leg a
little, and she then saw the open box of dressings on the
edge of his bed that she had quickly passed over earlier. "I
can't believe this is a social call, so I presume you do have a
purpose for being here."

Rachel drew a deep breath as he seated himself on the
side of the bed. He picked up a pair of scissors, and while
she watched in unwilling fascination, he cut off a length of

the fine pliable material to make a pad that would serve as a protection for the injury. He seemed totally indifferent to her presence there, neither disconcerted nor embarrassed by her attention, while she was a mass of taut nervous energy, tormented by the sympathy she was badly trying to conceal.

Jaime put the pad over the raw line of stitches that still oozed moisture as he moved. Evidently his leg was not healing as rapidly as it should with the demands he persistently made upon it, and Rachel itched to examine it, to ensure herself it was not festering.

Then he reached for the bandage he had discarded earlier, but as if becoming aware of her eyes still watching him, he looked up at her half impatiently. "What do you want, Rachel?" he asked shortly, obviously in some pain. "I can do without an audience while I'm doing this, so do you mind saying what you have to say and going?"

Rachel caught her lower lip between her teeth. "It looks...nasty," she ventured, her words in no way answering his demands, and his mouth compressed into a thin line.

"It is nasty," he declared flatly. "Bullet wounds are not known for their appearance. And don't tell me my mother sent you to dress it for me in her absence. I can put up with some things, but that's the outside of enough!"

Rachel frowned. "Your mother usually dresses it for you?"

"She winds on the bandage," Jaime admitted dryly. "It isn't in the easiest position for me to handle myself. But don't worry, I can do it, so your assistance isn't needed."

Rachel hesitated for a moment, and then walked slowly across to him, going down on her knees beside him, and grasping the end of the bandage. "I'll do it," she said, and when it seemed as if he was going to ignore her, she schooled her features and looked up at him. "Let me," she insisted. "It's the least you can do now that I'm here."

Jaime let go of the bandage abruptly, but his features were angry and tightly drawn. "What the hell does my mother think I am?" he muttered savagely. "I may be immobilized, but I'm not impotent!"

Rachel concentrated on what she was doing, not responding to his furious outburst. Instead, she lifted the pad he had placed earlier, and examined the wound for herself. At close quarters, she could see the knotted stitching, holding the flesh together, and after insuring that it was clean and not suppurating, she replaced the pad again.

"What do you think you're doing?" Jaime shifted impatiently on the bed. "For God's sake, put the bandage on, will you, and be done with it. I can't wait to see my mother and tell her what I think of her!"

Rachel began winding the bandage around his thigh, keeping it firm and crease-free and not too tight. "As...as a matter of fact, your mother didn't send me in here," she admitted reluctantly as she neared the end of the roll. "I...I came to return your ring, and...and you jumped to the wrong conclusion."

Jaime stared at her ominously. "So why are you doing it?"

"Someone had to." Rachel was defensive. "And...and I didn't think you'd mind, as...as you're obviously not perturbed about me seeing you in...in only—"

"My underwear?" he finished dryly, and Rachel nodded. "So why should I be perturbed about that?" he countered. "You've seen me often enough without it."

"I know." Rachel didn't want to get involved in that kind of conversation. "Anyway," she strove desperately to find an alternative. "It's finished now. Does it—I mean—it feels all right, doesn't it? Not too tight or anything."

Jaime looked at her for a long disturbing moment, and then flopped back resignedly on the bed. "No. No. It's okay," he assured her expressionlessly. "Honestly, the district nurse couldn't have done better."

"Good." Rachel got to her feet and looked down at him. "Well, I'd better be going then. I . . . I have to get ready for the party."

"The party! My God, yes, the party!" Jaime grimaced. "Do you think anyone would notice if I didn't turn up?"

"You're not serious!" Rachel gazed at him anxiously. "You know your mother would be upset."

"No, I'm not serious," agreed Jaime wearily, propping himself up on one elbow, and Rachel's tongue circled her lips doubtfully.

"You . . . you feel all right, don't you?" she ventured, aware of his pallor. "I mean—you're not feeling sick or headachy?"

"No."

Jaime spoke flatly, and Rachel sighed. "How . . . how did it happen?" she exclaimed. "Aren't news teams supposed to be protected or something? You don't carry any weapons, so why did they shoot you?"

Jaime considered for a moment. Then he shrugged.

"They didn't aim at us exactly," he said. "Didn't my mother tell you? We were caught in the crossfire between the government forces and the guerrillas. I suppose it was fortunate we were captured by the government forces. I don't believe the rebel army carries any wounded."

"You mean they might have killed you!" Rachel was horrified.

"Well, they might have tried to use us as hostages at first," Jaime reflected. "To try and get some of their men released from prison."

"And if they couldn't they would have killed you?"

"It's all speculation," said Jaime, sounding bored now. "It didn't happen that way, and in any case, what's it to you?" He rolled onto his back again. "I might as well be dead."

"No!" Rachel spoke vehemently, and he turned onto his side to look at her.

"No?" One dark brow quirked. "Why not? We never see one another, so what does it matter?"

Rachel clenched her fists. "I don't wish you dead."

"Don't you?"

"No." She gazed at him mutinously. "You should take better care of yourself. Your...your mother worries; you know she does."

Jaime expelled his breath on a sigh. "I'll bear that in mind."

"I wish you would."

"I will."

Jaime was looking tense now, and Rachel moved toward the door. "The, er, the ring's there," she said, indicating the box on the table beside the bed. "I, er, I'll see you at dinner—"

"Wait!" Jaime levered himself upright as she halted uncertainly. "Take the ring with you. I want you to keep it."

"No."

"Yes." He reached for the box and held it out to her. "It's yours."

Rachel put her hands behind her back. "I . . . I can't take a gift like that from you."

"Because it's too valuable? Yes, you said. Or is it because you don't believe I bought it for you?"

"You didn't." Rachel's mouth quivered. "You said so. And I . . . I'd as soon not wear something you bought for Betsy."

"I didn't buy it for Betsy," he snapped, aroused now. "And why can't you wear it? Don't you think you've earned it?"

"That's a rotten thing to say."

"I feel rotten," he retorted coldly. "Okay." He tossed the box carelessly onto the bed, and its contents spilled onto the coverlet. "Forget it! I'll get rid of it some other way."

Rachel hovered uneasily. "You . . . you have no right to criticize me—"

"Don't I?" He rolled onto his side facing away from her. "Go away, will you? I'm tired of this conversation."

Rachel opened the door, reluctantly aware that he had won this particular encounter. How was it that he could make her feel like a heel, when it was he who was responsible for this impossible situation? She slammed his door behind her with a little display of temper, and then glanced around her apprehensively as she realized how compromisingly she had drawn attention to herself.

In her own room she expelled her breath in a sigh of frustration. The idea of showering and changing, and getting ready for a dinner party had never seemed more undesirable, and she flung herself onto her own bed in a gesture of revolt. Jaime thought he could say what he liked to her, treat her with as little respect as a . . . a . . . ? Her mind balked at the inevitable conclusion. Well, she would make sure he did not have another opportunity. In future she would keep out of his way, and any sympathy she felt she would obliterate.

She felt a little better after that, and by the time she had showered and dried her hair, she was beginning to anticipate the evening ahead with some degree of enthusiasm. At least, in company, she could forget the emptiness of the future, and maybe this experience with Jaime would accomplish what time had not—to rid her of any lingering regrets for their separation.

She applied a delicate makeup, accentuating the slight tilt at the corners of her eyes, and outlining her mouth with a glossy brick-colored lipstick. Then, after brushing her hair into its silky shoulder-length curve, she picked up the dress she was going to wear.

It, too, was silky, a plain dull red sheath with a low V above its wrapover neckline, elbow length sleeves, and a clinging skirt that was slit almost the length of her thigh. It was certainly one of the most sophisticated dresses she had ever possessed, and its deceptively simple lines drew atten-

tion to the curve of her full breasts, and revealed the shapeliness of her long slender legs. She looked good and she
knew it, and for once she was glad to shelter behind the
shield of her beauty.

She heard a car arrive as she was dressing, and guessed
the Hyltons were here. Remembering what Liz had said
about their daughter being the same age as she was, she
decided she had better go down and allow Liz the chance to
change if she had not already done so. She doubted Nancy
would make the effort, and as she was ready, she might just
as well.

As she had suspected, Liz and Robert were entertaining
their guests in the sitting room. Maisie had provided tea,
but when Rachel entered the room Liz looked up gratefully.

"Oh, there you are, my dear," she exclaimed, as Robert
and Bernard Hylton got politely to their feet. "Come and
join us. I want you to meet Angela."

Bernard Hylton was a little like Robert, tall and burly, but
with a bristling ginger mustache. His wife, Alice, was tall,
too, but painfully thin, and evidently much in awe of her
aggressive husband.

Angela Hylton resembled neither of them. She was of
average height and build, with a mass of curling red hair
that surrounded her pale face like a fiery aureole. She was
pretty in a brittle, snapping kind of way, and Rachel knew,
without her even opening her mouth, that she and Angela
were unlikely allies.

"Angela is a model," remarked Liz after the introduc-
tions were over. "She's been all over the world in the
course of her work, haven't you, Angela?"

"Well, almost."

Angela spoke in a breathless girlish voice that Rachel immediately detested, and then chided herself for doing so. After all, Angela was nothing to her. She had no reason to judge the girl so harshly. There was just something about her that seemed to set Rachel's teeth on edge.

As she had expected, Liz made her excuses and went to change, and as the two men were discussing business matters, Rachel endeavored to play hostess.

"Do you live near here, Mrs. Hylton?" she asked politely, and Alice Hylton gave a small smile. Away from her husband, she was still rather reticent, but she admitted that actually they lived just outside of Newcastle.

"But we always come to Liz and Robert's on Christmas Day," she said. "And usually they come to us at New Year's."

"How nice." Rachel acknowledged this with an inclination of her head. "Christmas is a time for traditions."

"You haven't spent Christmas at Clere Heights before, have you, Miss Williams?" Angela asked, her hands clasped around her knees, and Rachel had to concede that she hadn't.

"But my father died earlier this year, and Liz and Robert knew I'd be on my own."

"In London?" Angela made a moue with her lips. "Is one ever alone in London?"

"One can be," replied Rachel smoothly, ignoring the bland criticism. "Do you always spend Christmas with your family, Miss Hylton?"

"Not always." Angela's lips tightened. "But when I

heard that Jaime was home, I couldn't wait to see him.''

Rachel rode this unexpected blow and forced an expression of mild interest. "Do you know Jaime well?"

"Of course." Angela's tone was scornful now. "I've known him since I was about six years old! He used to tease me abominably!"

"Angela used to follow him around like a shadow," Alice Hylton remarked, looking affectionately at her daughter. "She and Robin were always getting into mischief because of Jaime."

Rachel pressed her lips together. The picture of the young Angela trailing in Jaime's footsteps was not a palatable one, in spite of her professed disinterest, and for once she was quite relieved to remember that it was Betsy whom he had married.

"Where are the boys?" Angela inquired now, and Rachel's skin prickled at the familiar intonation. She wondered how much Liz had told the Hyltons of her involvement, and whether indeed Angela had any knowledge of her relationship with the Shard's elder son.

"Robin and Nancy will be down in a few minutes." It was Robert who broke in then, after overhearing Angela's query. "I expect you're dying to see my granddaughter, aren't you, Alice? I bet you didn't think we'd beat you to being grandparents."

Alice looked shyly embarrassed, and her husband spoke for her. "Well, it's true Angela has been engaged a couple of times, Rob, but I guess she's still looking for the right man." He shrugged. "As for Colin, he's married, as you know, but his wife seems determined to carry on with her career, and I can't see them having a family in the near future."

"What does your daughter-in-law do?" asked Rachel in the silence that followed, and Bernard gave her a friendly grin.

"She's a doctor, Miss Williams. At the infirmary in Newcastle. She's a clever girl, and I think we were all surprised when she accepted our Colin."

"Colin's not an idiot, dad!" Angela exclaimed with some asperity, and her father laughed.

"No, he's not," he admitted good-naturedly. "But running a string of race horses can't be compared to practicing medicine, now can it?"

"No. Owning race horses is more profitable," retorted Angela, and her father shook his head.

"I think Barbara should think again," remarked Alice, unexpectedly entering the discussion. "A woman's place is with her husband. His wishes should come first. That's why so many marriages fail nowadays. Too many women want to have their cake and eat it."

"Oh, I think a woman should pursue a worthwhile career, if that's what she wants," put in Rachel firmly. "A lot of marriages fail because the wife is bored and looks elsewhere for diversion. It's better to share your wife with her work, rather than with another man."

"A sage comment," remarked a lazy voice from the doorway; and Angela's squeal of delight saved Rachel's blushes.

"Jaime! Oh, Jaime, there you are!" She left her chair to fling herself across the room at him, and his murmur of protest was stifled by the intimate pressure of her lips.

"Darling! How are you?" she added huskily as he endeavored to keep his balance against the door frame. "You are a beast, you know. Frightening us all like that."

Rachel averted her eyes from the sight of Angela's dewy look of supplication. With Jaime's arm around her, as much to support himself as to embrace her, Rachel acknowledged candidly that Angela was nevertheless taking advantage of her opportunities, and her scarlet-tipped fingers rested against the pleated front of his shirt, her arm linked familiarly with his.

"I didn't know you cared," Jaime was remarking now, nodding across at her father and mother. "How are you, Bernard?" he greeted the older man politely. "Hello, Alice. You look well."

"It's you we're worried about," exclaimed Angela in the silly girlish voice that Rachel was beginning to dislike more and more.

"Oh, you don't have to worry about him," put in Robert dryly. "He's got more lives than a cat."

"Well, he's like a cat, aren't you, darling?" Angela insisted coyly. "Only not the tame domestic variety—a big sleek panther—"

"Would anyone like a drink?" suggested Robert, getting to his feet, and Rachel looked up at him gratefully.

"Yes," she said succinctly. "I'd like to try some of that contraband whiskey, Rob. That is, if you've got any left."

"Oh, I think I might be able to find you a drop, Rachel," he assured her kindly, and as he went to examine the contents of the liquor cabinet, Jaime eased himself into an armchair.

"War wounded," he observed mockingly by way of an apology to Angela, but she perched herself possessively on the arm of the chair beside him and conducted a conversation with him in low, inaudible tones.

Rachel glanced toward them impatiently, reluctantly aware of how attractive Jaime looked in the black pants and maroon velvet jacket he was wearing. With his hair smoothly combed and his tie expertly knotted, he looked much different from the last time she had seen him on his bed, but the memory of that lingered, and mocked her affirmed detachment.

When he turned his head and found her watching them, he bowed his head almost imperceptibly, and she looked down quickly at her hands. Dear God, was she going to have to add jealousy to the list of emotions he had inspired in her, and if so, what on earth was she going to do about it?

Robert supplied her with a generous measure of Scotch, and she drank the raw spirit eagerly. Its potency was numbing as well as deliciously warming, and by the time she reached the bottom of the glass, she was feeling infinitely more optimistic.

Robin and his wife had joined them by this time, and as everyone wanted to see the baby, Nancy was in her element. In a cowl-necked dress of apricot jersey, she looked the epitome of fulfilled womanhood, and Liz and Robert were obviously very thrilled to show the Hyltons their granddaughter.

"I see Angie baby hasn't wasted any time," remarked Robin, seating himself beside Rachel on the couch. "Did you know that she's been after him for years, but in spite of his marriage and her two broken engagements, she doesn't seem to be any further forward."

"I wouldn't say that," Rachel said carelessly, and then wished she hadn't as Robin's brows arched inquisitively. "Oh, well, I only meant she seems to know him—"

"Intimately?" supplied Robin dryly. "Don't you believe it. Jaime wouldn't get himself involved with a psycho like her." He grimaced. "Not after Betsy, anyway."

"What do you mean?" Rachel looked bewildered, and Robin shook his head.

"Nothing," he said flatly. "Forget I said it. Hey—that's a pretty dress you're almost wearing."

Rachel parried his habitual efforts to make a pass at her, and then the doorbell rang again to herald the vicar's and his wife's arrival, and more drinks were circulated. In the general melee, Rachel had no time to consider what Robin might have meant by his remark, and as the evening wore on it lost its significance.

The Mannings arrived, and with them their son, Patrick, who turned out to be an amateur musician. He had brought his guitar with him, and as Robert had rolled back the carpet in the hall for dancing later, it promised to be an entertaining evening.

Rachel's head was already feeling a little fuzzy by the time they sat down to dinner. With every new arrival, Robert had produced a round of drinks, and as Angela continued to monopolize Jaime, Rachel took refuge in her glass.

At dinner she was seated between Patrick Manning and the vicar, with Jaime diagonally opposite. He was sitting near the end of the table, with Angela between him and his

father, while Liz had Robin at the other end of the table, and Nancy only two seats away. None of the women, Rachel observed, had been placed beside their husbands, and she presumed Liz's arrangement of putting Jaime with Angela was designed to make it easier for her. But it didn't. It made it harder. And harder still when Jaime met her eyes without a trace of warmth in his.

The meal was the traditional one with an enormous roast turkey and a flaming plum pudding, and hot mince pies to finish. There were various wines served with the food, and brandy to add to the coffee, and Rachel was hardly surprised when she got up from the table to find that the room was spinning.

She offered to help Liz and Maisie carry the dishes away, glad of the exercise to clear her head, and by the time she returned to the sitting room, Patrick was playing carols on his guitar. Everyone was joining in, she noticed, squeezing unobtrusively into a corner, and with the lights extinguished and only firelight to illuminate the room, it was a very Christmassy scene.

"What do you think of Angela?" whispered Nancy, beside her, free now that Lisa had been settled down for the night in the Armstrong's bedroom. "Robin says that she's a model, but I can't think of what," she added cattily. "Unless, it's nail polish!"

Rachel's lips twitched. "Have you met her before?"

"Oh, yes." Nancy grimaced, evidently regarding Rachel with less hostility since their chat during their walk that morning. "I used to think she fancied Robin, until I saw her with Jaime."

Rachel's stomach fluttered uncomfortably. "Do you think Jaime fancies her?" she asked, and then chided herself for allowing the amount of alcohol she had consumed to dictate what she said, but Nancy was not perturbed.

"I don't know," she murmured, shrugging her shoulders. "But that's not always important, is it? I mean, if a girl fancies a man, he'd be a fool not to, wouldn't he?"

Rachel gasped. "You mean—you think that any man would—"

"Well, wouldn't you?" Nancy purred. "After all, it's not the same for a man, is it? Just a...fact of life."

Rachel said no more. Nancy was probably right, she decided bitterly. After what Jaime had said to her that afternoon, she should know better than to argue. But that didn't stop the awful aching feeling inside her, or relieve the tension that was tying her up in knots.

When Patrick stopped playing and the lights were restored, Robert put a record on the stereo and set the ball rolling by leading Mrs. Manning onto the hall's polished floor. It encouraged the Conways to join them, and Bernard Hylton gallantly partnered Liz.

"D'you want to dance?"

Rachel looked up in surprise to find Patrick in front of her, looking rather bashful at having to invite her in front of Nancy.

"Oh—I—if you like," she responded, offering him her hand, and he pulled her up confidently and steered her out into the hall.

Unlike everyone else, he was not wearing a dinner jacket, but his rather rakish good looks complemented the jeans and sweater he was wearing. He was younger than she was, Rachel guessed, barely twenty-one or -two, and evidently out of his element in this kind of gathering.

"I'm not much good, really," he confessed when they reached the edge of the dance floor. "This kind of gig isn't my line, but I'm willing to take a chance if you are."

"I've never had a better offer," said Rachel with a soft laugh. "I'm no ballroom dancer, either, so we should suit one another."

"Okay."

Patrick grinned and pulled her close, and they moved in slow rhythm with the music. It was a slow fox trot, or so Robert had announced, but they were all the same to Patrick, and when the beat changed to a waltz, they hardly altered their step.

It was only when Robin interfered with his father's planning and put a modern group on the record deck that Patrick came to life, and Rachel was relieved her skirt had a slit in the side as he started to spin her around.

"Good old rock and roll," he said as he pulled her against him. "You're good, do you know that? Hey, this is great!"

"I had a good teacher," said Rachel breathlessly, whirling on her heels, and then became aware that their exhibition was attracting everyone else's attention. As well as the older couples, Jaime and Angela had come to stand in the doorway leading from the sitting room, and Rachel wondered giddily whether he had heard what she had said. Jaime had taught her everything she knew about dancing, both disco and modern, and she had to force herself to concentrate on Patrick as she felt Jaime's eyes upon her

When the music stopped she was breathless, and he head was still whirling. It had been an exhilarating experience, but now that it was over, she wondered if she had been exactly wise to participate.

"You need a drink," said Patrick firmly, imprisoning he within the circle of his arms. "I know a nice little corne where we can share a beer, and you can tell me your life story. And later on, if there's time, I'll tell you mine."

Rachel was feeling hot and uncomfortable, and she pushed futilely at his sweating chest. "Really—I don't thin that's at all a good idea," she said, trying to free herself "Let me go, Patrick. I don't feel very well."

"Aw, c'mon." Patrick bent his face unpleasantly close to hers. "I'm not threatening your virtue or anything. I jus want us to spend a little time together. As the only youn people here, I think we owe it to each other."

"Patrick—"

"My turn, I think," inserted Jaime curtly, cutting be tween them with grim determination. Without too much effort, he set Rachel free, and then countered Patrick's ag gression with a hard-eyed smile.

"The lady's tired," said Patrick, facing him out. "She wants a drink."

"Later," said Jaime, his hand descending on Rachel' arm, and the younger man had little choice but to accept the situation.

Rachel, for her part, was amazed at how relieved she felt to see Jaime. He had left Angela, where Rachel had las seen them together, and was supporting himself unaided though he favored his left leg. Remembering the gash she had seen in his thigh, Rachel was both shocked and reluctantly anxious, and after Patrick had departed with ill grace, she turned to thank him.

"Dance," said Jaime grimly, pulling her toward him, and she gazed up at him uncomprehendingly as his arms slipped around her.

"You...you can't," she protested, looking down at his leg, but Jaime just ignored her as they moved in time to the slow rhythm.

"You want to start a fight?" he inquired, keeping a couple of inches between them, and Rachel fingered his lapel.

"I don't understand—"

"If Manning thought I was being heavy-handed, he might conceivably turn nasty." Jaime shrugged. "So we dance. For a few minutes, anyway."

Rachel sighed, pursing her lips as she looked up at him. "And won't your girl friend mind? Your deserting her for me, I mean?"

"Who? Angela?" Jaime grimaced. "I guess she thinks she has nothing to worry about."

Rachel gazed at him resentfully. "I suppose you told her she hasn't. So long as you're holding me at arm's length, anyway. What's the matter? Am I contaminated or something? Or are you afraid of what I might do to you?"

Jaime's eyes were cold. "I think you've had too much to drink," he declared flatly. "I watched you swallowing those Scotches before dinner. I knew then you were asking for trouble, but of course you knew better."

"How would you know what I was doing?" she demanded angrily. "You were too engrossed with Angela. Drooling all over her, you were. It was disgusting!"

"Was it?" He was contemptuous. "Well, I suggest you mind your own business in future, hmm?"

"I will. Oh, I will."

"I'm glad to hear it." Jaime stopped abruptly and glanced around. "Well, it seems that your errant swain has disappeared. I guess we can call it a day, don't you?"

"If you like."

Rachel was hurt and indignant, but as Jaime turned away, she had to reach for him again with urgent fingers. The room was revolving slowly around her, and she panicked as a terrible nausea rose into her throat.

CHAPTER SEVEN

"WHAT IS IT?"

Jaime looked impatient as he turned back to her, but at the sight of her pallid face, his irritation fled. With a muffled oath he stepped in front of her, shielding her from the rest of the dancers, and looked down at her frustratedly as she swayed unsteadily before him.

"I feel awful!" she moaned, pressing her hot face against his shoulder, and with a sharp expellation of his breath, he put his arm around her.

"Come on," he said grimly. "You can make it up the stairs. You don't want to make a fool of yourself down here, do you? Not in front of Patrick...and Angela!"

Rachel was vaguely aware of Liz hurrying toward them as they walked to the stairs, but Jaime gestured her to stay away. Then she felt the cooler air fanning her forehead as they mounted to the first landing, and saw the lamplit corridor wavering ahead of her.

Jaime pushed open the door of her room, and the sickness she had been steeling not to break got the better of her. Dragging herself away from him, she staggered dizzily into the bathroom, and disgraced herself completely in the rose-patterned basin.

She seemed to lean there for ages while retching wracked her body, and the dizziness slowly subsided. But it was replaced by a terrible feeling of humiliation that was not helped when she turned and found Jaime leaning against the door frame watching her.

"Here." He passed her his handkerchief as she straightened, and she wiped her mouth without looking at him. "Are you feeling better? You still look as white as a sheet."

"I'm sorry." Rachel kicked off her shoes, and padded past him into the bedroom. "I'm sorry I had to involve you in all this." She sat down on the side of the bed. "Apologize to your parents for me."

"I think Liz got the picture," remarked Jaime dryly, rubbing his leg painfully as he came into the room. "It's after eleven o'clock, anyway. The party will soon be over. My parents don't go in for all-night festivities."

Rachel looked up at him unhappily. "Your leg! You must be in agony! You haven't even got your cane."

"I'm not exactly incapacitated," retorted Jaime wryly. "Now, are you going to be all right?"

Rachel nodded. "I'm going to bed," she said, suddenly aware of their isolation in the lamplit room. She stood up abruptly, to dispel the illusion, and then lost her balance ignominiously so that he had to save her from falling.

"Come on," he said huskily. "I'll help you." His hands found the zipper at the back of her dress. "Relax, I'm not going to touch you. I just want to make sure you don't do yourself an injury."

Rachel hadn't the strength to obstruct him, and besides, she was beginning to feel very sleepy, and she couldn't wait to put her head on the cool pillow. She let Jaime remove her dress, and then stretched lazily on the creamy silk sheets while he took off her stockings.

"I'll leave you to do the rest," he said harshly, tossing the shreds of nylon aside, and Rachel looked up at him below heavy lids.

"I...I haven't thanked you," she said, but he pressed his hand down in a gesture of dismissal.

"There's no need," he muttered. "I'll leave you now. I—well, if you need anything, just shout. Somebody's bound to hear you."

"All right." Rachel wanted to detain him, but she knew it would be crazy, so she raised herself on her elbows and smiled. "I...I am grateful, anyway." She paused. "Say goodbye to the Hyltons for me."

"You'll see them tomorrow," retorted Jaime abruptly, opening the bedroom door. "Didn't my mother explain that they usually stay the night? So that Bernard doesn't drink and drive."

"Oh!" Rachel's mouth tightened. So Angela would have her chance. "All right, then. See you in the morning!" and she curled into a ball as he went out the door.

Funnily enough, as soon as he had gone, her tiredness left her. Maybe it was the knowledge of knowing that Angela was going to spend the night in the house that had aroused her, but whatever it was, she was fully wide-awake.

Her mouth tasted vile, and sliding out of bed again, she steadied herself before staggering into the bathroom once more. Toothpaste had never tasted sweeter, and her breath was sweet and peppermint-scented before she rinsed her face and hands.

Grimacing at her appearance in lacy bra and panties, she

tossed them off and pulled on her green satin nightdress. Then, after brushing her hair thoroughly, she climbed back into bed and turned out the lamp.

Immediately the awful dizziness returned, and she groped for the light switch and turned it on again. Darkness was obviously something to be avoided, she decided, but it wasn't easy trying to sleep with the lamp on.

As she lay there, she heard the sounds of the party subsiding, and presently the revving of engines as the Shards' guests departed. The Conways went first, then the Mannings, and eventually she heard the sound of footsteps on the stairs, and Robin and Nancy saying good-night to his parents. There was the murmur of unfamiliar voices as Liz showed the Hyltons and Angela to their rooms, and finally the deeper murmur of Jaime's voice as he exchanged a few words with his mother.

Then silence.

Rachel shifted a little restlessly, wondering whether Jaime had said good-night to Angela yet. One thing was certain, she thought bitterly, he would not need to seek oblivion in a bottle of Scotch with such an open invitation only waiting to be accepted. Her lips quivered at the unwelcome image of Angela and Jaime together. Even if she did not want him, she resented having to watch his developing relationship with another woman....

When her door was silently opened, she thought for a moment that Liz had come to see if she was all right. But it wasn't Jaime's mother, who looked into the room, but Jaime himself, and Rachel's breathing almost stopped altogether.

When he saw she was still awake, a curiously impatient expression crossed his face, but after glancing behind him, he let himself into the room and pushed the door almost shut behind him.

"I saw the light," he explained. "I thought you must have fallen asleep and left it on. I was going to turn it out for you."

"How kind."

After her thoughts of a few moments before, Rachel didn't find it easy being friendly toward him, and his expression grew speculative.

"What's wrong?"

"Nothing." Rachel moved her shoulders beneath the covers. "What could be wrong?"

"Then why isn't the light out?"

"Because—oh, because I felt dizzy when I turned it out."

"I see." Jaime frowned. "You don't feel dizzy now?"

"I don't know, do I? I . . . I haven't tried it again."

Jaime hesitated. "But you're okay?"

"Yes."

"Good." With a helpless shrug, he turned back toward the door, leaning heavily on the cane he had brought with him this time, and Rachel pursed her lips.

"Are you?" she asked unwillingly. "Is your leg painful?"

"I can cope," he replied dryly, and indignation made her reckless.

"I bet you can," she muttered bitterly, and his dark brows descended.

"I beg your pardon?"

Rachel sniffed, but she had to go on. "Don't let me keep you."

"Keep me?" Jaime looked puzzled. "Keep me from what?"

"Don't pretend you don't know." Rachel spoke resentfully. "I'd hate to play gooseberry."

"What the hell are you talking about?" he demanded, turning back to her now, and as he met her sulky green eyes, comprehension dawned. "My God!" He uttered an angry ejaculation. "Are you still bugging me about Angela? Dammit, what do you think I am? Some kind of stud?"

"Aren't you?"

Jaime's eyes smoldered. "I should thrash you for saying a thing like that." He made a gesture of disgust. "I don't know why I concern myself about you."

"Why you concern yourself about me?" Rachel propped herself up on her elbow, and as she did so, the bedcovers slipped back to expose the creamy line of her shoulders emerging from the narrow straps of her nightgown.

"Yes." His mouth twisted. "Oh, go to sleep! It's too late, and I'm too weary to have this kind of an argument!"

Rachel knew a pang of regret as he moved toward the door. Almost in spite of herself she believed him when he denied an involvement with Angela. The trouble was, she didn't trust Angela . . . or Jaime's reactions now she had accused him.

"Jaime!"

Her whispered use of his name arrested him, and he glanced around at her suspiciously as he reached for the door. "Well?"

"I'm sorry," she said, replacing a strap that had slipped off her shoulder. "I am sorry, honestly. Please...don't go."

"Don't go?" His expression was ludicrous, a mixture of disbelief, anger and pure frustration, and she gave him an appealing look.

"The dizziness," she said. "It...it frightens me. Couldn't you stay for a little while? Just until I fall asleep?"

Jaime closed the door with precise constrained movements, and then turned to face her, tight-lipped. "You have to be crazy!" he told her savagely. "What do you think I am?"

"I thought you were my friend," she murmured plaintively, affecting Angela's childlike innocence, and his free fist clenched ominously.

"We can never be friends, Rachel," he snapped violently, and then realizing his voice might be overheard, he came nearer the bed. "Leave the light on," he advised, supporting himself stiffly on his cane. "I doubt if it will bankrupt my father, and if it means you'll have a good night's rest—"

"But I won't," she exclaimed, not quite knowing why she was doing this, but driven to it all the same. "I mean—I can't sleep with the light on, you know that. Couldn't you...couldn't you turn it out for me, and just...sit by the bed until I go to sleep?"

Jaime's mouth compressed. "What kind of a game do you think you're playing?"

"No game!" Rachel's eyes were wide. "Please! I hate the dizziness."

Jaime looked as if he would refuse, but his leg was evidently hurting him, and after a moment's inner conflict he flung himself into the basket chair beside her. "All right," he said, extinguishing the light without ceremony. "Now, go to sleep or I leave."

"Give me your hand."

Rachel lowered herself back onto the pillows carefully, relieved to find she no longer felt dizzy, and after a moment Jaime's firm fingers found hers.

"Good night," she murmured softly, deciding to keep him there for no longer than half an hour, and closed her eyes peacefully, amazingly content.

SHE AWAKENED to the gray light of a winter's dawn and to the uneasy sensation that all was not well. Her head ached a little, but it wasn't that that troubled her. It was something else, something she should have remembered, and as she shifted beneath the covers, she encountered an unexpectedly solid object.

She turned her head quickly, unable at first to distinguish who or what it was beside her, and then blinked her eyes disbelievingly at the sight of Jaime's soundly slumbering form. In an instant the events of the night before came back to her in hazy detail, and although she closed her eyes against their memory, the evident result of her recklessness was there beside her. Dear God, what had happened after Jaime came to her room? If only she could remember. But all she could recall was the argument they had had, and his hand holding hers before she fell asleep.

She expelled her breath a little unsteadily and stretched her legs, tentatively investigating what she was wearing. She breathed somewhat easier when she discovered she still had on her nightdress, and shifting her weight carefully, she turned on her side to look at Jaime.

The brown skin of his shoulders, exposed above the sheet, was disturbing, and on impulse, she stretched a hand toward him, her fingers brushing his bare leg only inches away from hers. But above the bandage, her hand encountered the cotton hem of his trunks, and her investigations ceased when his eyes flickered open.

"Rachel?" he muttered, his brown eyes confused, and then, as comprehension dawned, he thrust her hand away saying harshly, "What the hell do you think you're doing?"

"I...I could ask you that question," she exclaimed, momentarily unnerved by his aggression. "What...what are you doing here? Did I...did I invite you into my bed?"

Jaime brought the watch on his wrist up to his eyes, and after ascertaining that it was barely seven o'clock, he looked at her through narrowed lids. "Don't you remember?"

Rachel's lips pursed. "If I did, I wouldn't be asking you, would I?" she retorted crossly. She circled her lips with a thoughtful finger. "I remember going to bed, I remember you coming in here—"

"But nothing else?" Jaime was mocking.

"I'm not sure." Rachel was loath to give him any further advantage. Then, summoning what little dignity was left to her, she said, "Anyway, you had no right to stay with me, whatever I said—did. You knew I had had too much to drink. I didn't know what I was doing."

Jaime shrugged, stretching indolently beside her, "There's a pity!" he taunted, and Rachel propped herself up on one elbow to look down at him.

"What . . . what did happen?" she pleaded, unable to sustain her indignation when inside she was in turmoil. "I—I—why did you stay here?" She moved her legs restlessly. "Did we make love?"

Jaime turned his head to look at her. "Don't you know?"

Rachel sighed. "Well, I don't feel—that is, oh, how can I be sure? Jaime, please—"

"You fell asleep holding my hand," he declared flatly. "I think I dozed, too." He paused. "Anyway, when I came around, I was freezing, and as I didn't fancy going back to my cold bed, I decided to share yours."

Rachel gasped, and now that she could breathe freely again, she was angry, too. "You . . . you had no right!"

"Probably not," he agreed. "But before you start berating me, remember, you invited me to stay."

"Not to *sleep* with me!"

"Why not?" He folded his arms behind his head. "As you wanted me to keep out of Angela's bed, it was the least you could do."

"You swine!" His sardonic indifference infuriated her, particularly as she was having to fight the subversive influence of his attraction. "I must have been mad to ask you for help!"

She turned abruptly, intent only on getting out of bed and putting a safe distance between them, when he reached for her. She struggled violently, managing to wrench her arm out of his grasp, but he caught a handful of her nightgown, the satin clinging to his fingers, and in its cloying folds, Rachel was like a butterfly in a net.

"Let go of me. Let go of me," she said through her

teeth, twisting and turning, and trying to kick him, but this time he gave her no chance to hurt him. He imprisoned her body beneath the weight of his, and when his lips found hers, she had no breath left to resist him.

"You should have known better than to provoke me in the morning, sweetness," he said against her mouth, as it opened to the insistent invasion of his tongue. "Particularly when you're in such a vulnerable situation. You know I only take what I've been offered."

"I haven't offered you anything!" she protested huskily, but her hands seemed to deny this, moving of their own accord over the muscled length of his back, so that a shudder ran through him.

"Rachel!" he muttered, his lips probing her ear, his tongue finding the sensitive hollow behind it. "Oh, Rachel, I want you, I want to be a part of you. Don't tell me no, because I don't think you could stop me now."

She wanted to object. She wanted to keep her head and push him away from her, but she didn't. When his hands disposed of the straps of her nightgown and pushed the bodice down to her waist, she let him, and she could only moan in sensual abandon when his mouth took possession of one of her breasts. No one but Jaime had ever made love to her, but he had taught her well the delights and desires of her own body and she found her emotions impossible to control.

The bedclothes were thrust aside, but they didn't heed the cooler air against their heated flesh. Following the line of her satin gown with his lips, he pressed it down the quivering length of her, and her traitorous body arched toward him.

She realized he was as naked as she was when the warmth of him surged against her, but by then she could no longer offer any protest. Only Jaime had ever been able to make her feel like this, to melt the cool exterior that concealed the passionate woman beneath, and in spite of everything that had gone before, everything she knew about him, she had to experience that sublime sensation one more time. In the early hours of the first night they had spent together, he had taught her the true meaning of making love, and after that, she had been as eager as he to share that intimate experience.

Now she was a woman, in every sense of the word, who had for too long been denied the completeness of surrender. She was hungry for him, and she wound herself around him eagerly, returning his caresses with all the instinctive sexuality of her young body. His mouth plundered her breasts, his tongue setting the downy skin on fire, inciting the flame that was growing inside her. She twisted and turned beneath him, bringing a groan of satisfaction from his lips, and then his mouth covered hers, opening it wide to his touch. Her senses surged to limitless peaks of pleasure. It was like being carried on a tide of physical sensation, and although the waves subsided, she was loath to let them go.

Her brain surfaced reluctantly through a misty cloud of satiation, and as the contours of the room came back into focus, so, too, did the horrifying disgrace of what she had done.

Jaime was still slumped beside her, one leg over both of hers. His arm, too, was draped possessively across her body, as if to restrain any ideas she might have of escaping from him, and as she attempted to move away from him, his drowsy lids lifted.

"That was good, wasn't it?" he said huskily, turning his mouth against her shoulder. "God, Rachel, how have I lived without you for so long? You're the only woman who can make me feel like this."

Rachel's jaw jutted. "Please. I don't want to talk about it."

"Why not?" Jaime aroused himself sufficiently to blink and open his eyes wide, though they were still glazed and drugged with sexual satisfaction. "What are you talking about, Rachel?" His mouth twisted wryly. "Surely you're not inhibited with me!" A faint smile tugged at his lips. "I wouldn't have thought it possible...now."

Rachel pushed his questing mouth away and struggled up onto the pillows, reluctant to pull the covers over her, even though she badly wanted to, because it would mean covering him, too.

"You don't understand," she said impatiently. "I don't want to talk about it...ever. I...I wish it had never happened."

"But it has," said Jaime flatly, rapidly getting the message and levering himself into an upright position. "And you're crazy if you think you can dismiss our relationship and pretend it's all over. What happened just now was as much your fault as mine!"

"So it was a fault, was it?"

"Damn you, you know what I mean," he snapped, and she knew he hated being forced to discuss it now. He was lethargic and heavy-eyed, and the exhaustion of two broken nights of sleep had painted dark rings around his eyes. "You're mine, Rachel. I put my mark upon you years ago, and now that I know how you really feel, no one is going to come between us, not even you!"

"That's what you think." Rachel jackknifed off the bed, snatched up the satin wrapper that went with her discarded nightgown, and wrapped it closely around her. "You may have possessed my body, but you haven't possessed my mind, and nothing... *nothing* you can do will change the way I feel about you."

Jaime expelled his breath in a heavy sigh, drawing up his uninjured leg, and resting his chin on it. "Oh, Rachel," he said wearily, "don't do this to me!"

"I... I'm not doing anything to you," she hissed, keeping her voice low just in case anyone had overheard them. "I don't know how you can sit there and pretend that I'm to blame! After... after the way you lied to me!"

Jaime tilted his head to look at her. "I didn't lie to you," he declared expressionlessly. "I didn't tell you I was married, but you didn't ask."

Rachel gasped. "Why should I? You didn't act like a married man."

"Because I didn't feel like one," Jaime retorted harshly. "Betsy and I were separated fifteen... eighteen months after the wedding! It was a fiasco!"

Rachel put her hands to her ears. "I don't want to hear."

"All right." Jaime moved his shoulders in a dismissing gesture. "That's typical of you. You get an idea into your head, and nothing anyone can say will move it."

"What could you say?" Rachel's hands dropped and she made a scornful gesture. "You were married. That's all there is to it. And... and you were living... living with *her*!"

"No!" Jaime fairly bounded off the bed then, only to

mutter a groaning imprecation as he jarred his wounded leg. 'Rachel, that's not true. I was not living with her. For God's sake, how could I be? Every spare minute I had, *we* spent together!"

Rachel turned aside from his male beauty, aware that even now he had the power to make her senses spin. There was a treacherous voice inside her that urged her to forget her grievances, at least until she left Clere Heights, but she knew it was only sex that was rearing its greedy head. If she allowed what had just happened to happen again, she would be that much weaker a second time, and sooner or later her body's needs might deafen her ears to the cool voice of reason. Somehow she had to resist him, and once she was back in London, away from his influence, time would achieve what common sense could not.

"I think you should go," she said, wrapping her arms around herself. "I... I've told you, we've said all there is to say."

"And you still think I was responsible for Betsy being pregnant?" he demanded grimly, and at her nod, continued, "Rachel, I swear to you by everything that's holy, that was not!"

"How can you say that?" She turned to him then, her lips parted incredulously. "Jaime, when you came back from Greece, you knew she had been to see me!"

"Yes."

He nodded, and she shook her head. "How?"

"She phoned me the minute I got back to the apartment. You must have told her I was due back—"

"No!"

"Well, the studios, maybe!" He was impatient. "Some

how she had got that knowledge, but not from me, and of course the first thing she told me about was the child.''

Rachel caught her breath. "You can stand there and tell me that?''

"Why not? It's the truth.''

"But—if you were not the father, why should she tell you? Wouldn't it have been more in keeping for her to tell the child's father?''

Jaime sighed. "You have to understand Betsy. Rachel, she's not like other women—''

"Obviously not.'' Rachel was so strung up, she didn't care who she hurt. "If I'd been her, I'd have been waiting for you with a shotgun! Either that or a hospital bill wrapped up in divorce papers!''

Jaime massaged the back of his neck wearily. "You're completely obstinate about this, aren't you? You won't even listen to my explanations.''

Rachel's chin wobbled. "Were you or were you not still married to her?''

"Yes. Yes, damn you. Yes!'' he snarled, and with an abrupt exclamation, he bent and hauled on the trousers of the dinner suit he had worn the night before. Zipping them to his waist, he put his arms into the sleeves of his shirt and pulled that on, also.

"Okay,'' he said. "I've had it. You win.'' He rescued the rest of his belongings where they had fallen and walked barefooted to the door. "I can't go on banging my head against a brick wall,'' he declared flatly. "After a certain length of time you forget why you started it, and once that happens, you begin to think it wasn't worth it.''

CHAPTER EIGHT

AFTER HE HAD LEFT, Rachel was shaking so much she had to sit down on the bed until she could control herself. The aftermath of Jaime's lovemaking combined with the awful scene that had followed had evoked a devastating reaction, and her limbs felt weak and on the point of collapse.

It didn't help to acknowledge that she was as much responsible for what had occurred as Jaime. It didn't prevent her from feeling a frustrated resentment that he should still have the power to overwhelm her inhibitions, to submerge her personality, and make her a willing supplicant to his desires. She should not have drunk so much the night before. She should not have invited him into her room. And she should not have been foolish enough to fall asleep in the company of a man without shame or integrity.

Yet that wasn't entirely true, either, she thought, chewing unhappily at her thumbnail. He had done nothing to her without her full knowledge, and last night, when she had been weak and vulnerable, he had shown her sympathy and compassion.

But for what purpose, she demanded of herself now. Had he intended this all along? But she dismissed this thought without consideration. Until she became jealous of his asso-

ciation with Angela, she had had no contact with him al
evening.

The fact remained that it had happened, and in spite o
her bitter turmoil, the haunting echoes of emotion woul
not be denied. Her body still throbbed at the memory o
Jaime's possession, and there were faintly red marks on he
skin where her chin was irritated.

With a feeling of tearful self-derision, she rolled into
ball on the bed and drew the tumbled covers over her. I
was too early yet to get up, too early yet to face the day, an
she was suddenly very sleepy. Pulling the coverlet over he
ears, she buried her face in the pillow, and although she wa
sure she would never rest, oblivion quickly claimed her.

SHE AWAKENED TO A SHAFT OF SUNLIGHT streaming through
the crack in the curtains, and to the realization that Maisi
was standing by the bed holding a tray.

"I thought I'd better disturb you, miss," she said as Ra
chel blinked rather absently up at her. "It's after eleven
and Mrs. Shard said as how you weren't too well last night."

Rachel closed her eyes again, and then opened them wit
a firm determination. "No. No, I wasn't, Mrs. Arm
strong," she responded, struggling up onto her pillows
"I . . . I must have been more tired than I thought."

"Yes, miss."

Maisie's expression was carefully impersonal, and Ra
chel, frowning as she endeavored to show a composed face
suddenly realized why. In her haste to sit up she had forgot
ten she was wearing only the satin negligee she had throw
about her to protect her naked form from Jaime's eyes, an

s she had not fastened the robe, it was now gaping reveal-
ngly.

"Oh!" Recognizing this fact, Rachel quickly drew the
wo sides of her robe together and offered the housekeeper
n apologetic smile. "I, er, I must have put my robe on in
nistake for my nightie."

"Would this be your nightdress, miss?"

Maisie set the tray across Rachel's semi-reclining form
nd bent to pick up the scrap of green satin on the floor
vhere Jaime had discarded it.

"What? Oh, oh, yes. So it is." Rachel refused to make
ny further explanations. "Thank you, Mrs. Armstrong.
Vould you just leave it on the end of the bed?"

"Right, miss." Maisie examined the nightgown briefly as
he folded it and laid it on the end of the bed. Then, after a
noment's hesitation when she seemed to be examining her
eet, she added, "Is there anything else I can get you?"

"No. No. This looks lovely." Rachel smiled her thanks
or the tray, on which sat orange juice, toast, cherry jam,
offee and fluted curls of butter on a transparent china dish.
'I, er, thank you, Mrs. Armstrong. Will you tell Mrs. Shard
'll be down in half an hour?"

"Very well, miss." Maisie moved toward the door. "It's
lovely morning. It's a shame to miss it."

"Yes." Rachel faltered for a moment, then she said,
'Is... is everyone else up?"

"All but Miss Hylton, miss," Maisie replied, folding her
ands. "Mr. and Mrs. Hylton had breakfast with Mr. and
Irs. Shard, and young Robin and his wife are having theirs
ist now."

"I see." Rachel caught her upper lip between her teeth. "And, er, and Jaime?"

"Didn't you know, miss?" Maisie genuinely looked surprised. "He left half an hour ago."

"Left?"

Rachel couldn't keep the consternation out of her voice, and Maisie nodded. "You knew he had a phone call from London, didn't you? From the studios?"

"No." Rachel could feel what little color she had draining out of her face.

"Well, he did." Maisie was disapproving. "It seems they need him to fly out to the United States to attend some high-level meetings there or something. Anyway, he said he'd go, even though his mother begged him to reconsider."

"But...his leg—"

"That's what his mother and father said, but he seemed to think he could cope. He said he was no invalid, and that in a job like his you learned to take life as it came." Maisie shrugged. "They sent a car to take him to the airport at Newcastle, and they've arranged a flight to take him to London."

"I see." Rachel felt curiously empty. "I didn't know."

"No. I can see that," responded Maisie dryly. "Have you got a headache or something. You're looking very pasty."

Rachel endeavored to pull herself together. "Oh—it's probably a hangover, Mrs. Armstrong," she murmured, determinedly picking up the coffeepot and pouring herself a cup of the hot black liquid. "I'll be all right when I've had this. You'll see."

Maisie left, but not without evident misgivings. Rachel

uessed she found her presence here at Clere Heights
omething of an enigma. In Maisie's world, one's son's ex-
irl-friends were not treated as friends of the family, and
lthough she seemed to like Rachel, no doubt she found
he whole situation slightly irregular.

Rachel drank her coffee, forced down half a slice of
oast, and then got out of bed. It was going to be easier,
he thought, knowing she did not have to face Jaime, but
he couldn't deny a troublesome sense of anxiety at the
nowledge he was on his way back to London. He should
ot have gone, she thought unhappily, and no doubt if
he had not been here, his mother would have offered
iore persuasion to keep him here. As it was, she felt like
ie cuckoo in the nest, and she wondered if she still had
ie nerve to carry it through after what had happened.

As she swung her feet to the floor, her toe encountered
omething soft and woolen that was definitely not the car-
et's pile. Frowning, she looked down, and then her shoul-
ers sagged as she recognized one of Jaime's dark socks. It
as lying half turned inside out, just where Maisie had res-
ued her nightgown, and remembering the housekeeper's
iomentary absorption with her toes, Rachel's face burned.
ear God, no wonder Maisie had expected her to know
here Jaime had gone! A sock was so unmistakable, and its
ieaning equally so.

As she took her shower and later dressed in jeans and a
weater, Rachel tried to decide what she ought to do. Was
laisie likely to tell her employer, and if so, was Liz likely to
iention it to her?

It was highly speculative, and hopefully unlikely, but the

fact remained, Maisie must know what had happened. To combine the sock with Rachel's own state of undress and the discarded nightgown lying on the floor constituted a watertight case in anyone's book, and Rachel didn't think she could stand anyone's censure or sympathy.

She carried her own tray downstairs and encountered Liz herself coming out of the kitchen. Jaime's mother smiled kindly at her and asked how she was feeling, and then, after explaining that the Hyltons would be leaving after lunch, she continued on about her business as if nothing untoward had happened. She neither mentioned Jaime nor his departure, and Rachel could only assume Maisie had admitted she had told her.

Maisie herself was busy at the sink, peeling the outer leaves from a dishful of sprouts. She smiled her thanks when Rachel set the tray down on the draining board, and asked her if she felt better now that she was up.

"I'm fine," said Rachel briefly, circling her tongue with her lips. "Er, is there anything I can do to help?"

"I don't think so." Maisie shook her head. "It's a cold meal for lunch. I thought some ham and cold sliced turkey, and a dish of tossed salad. These sprouts are for this evening. When there'll just be the family again."

Rachel nodded. "And me," she inserted quietly.

"Well . . . ." Maisie turned to look at her. "You're family, aren't you? Or almost."

"Not even almost," contradicted Rachel heavily. Then she added "Maisie, I know you saw that sock just now—"

"It's nothing to do with me, miss," declared Maisie, making no attempt to deny she knew what Rachel was talking about. "What you and Jaime do in your own time is not my affair."

Rachel sighed. "I just wanted you to know—"

"I mind my own business," said Maisie flatly, and then, as if feeling obliged to reassure her, she added, "I know Jaime, miss. I've known him since he was so high. And I know how he used to feel about you—"

"Maisie!"

For once Rachel forgot to be polite, but the housekeeper didn't appear to notice. "You listen to me," she said. "If you and he are getting back together, then I won't be the only one who's pleased. That one—" she gestured with her head, and Rachel knew she meant Liz "—she worries about him all the time, she does. What with that business over his wife, and all! Been nothing but a source of trouble to him, she has, and him only trying to do what's best for her."

Rachel knew she shouldn't get involved in a discussion about Betsy with Mrs. Armstrong, but her curiosity was such that she couldn't deny just one question. "Did... did you ever meet his wife, Mrs. Armstrong?" she asked tentatively, and was amazed at the look of bitterness that crossed the housekeeper's face.

"Oh, aye," she said, her knife tearing savagely into the vegetable in her hand. "I met her. Several times. He used to bring her here to Rothside, until that trouble with the Marshall boy."

"The Marshall boy?" Rachel was getting in deeper every minute.

"Yes. Terry Marshall. At the garage. Don't you know him?"

Rachel's mouth felt dry. "You mean... the young man Robert called the local Lothario?"

"That's him." Maisie grimaced, and then shook her head. "Well—after that, she wasn't welcome here anymore."

Rachel stared at the housekeeper's bent head, dying to ask what had happened to make Betsy unwelcome at Clere Heights, but there were limits to even her audacity. With a helpless gesture she turned away, and only as she reached the door did Maisie speak again.

"I won't tell Mrs. Shard, if that's what you're worried about," she declared perceptively, and Rachel bit her lip. "She's got enough to worry about as it is," she added obscurely, and Rachel could only offer a helpless word of thanks as she went out the door.

Lunch was a subdued meal with none of the previous evening's conviviality. Even Robin was slumped morosely in his seat, the reason for which became clear when Rachel accidentally overheard Angela's name used with some asperity by his wife in the living room afterward. Apparently after Jaime's disappearance with Rachel, the resourceful Angela had turned her attention on Robin, and knowing his susceptibility to a pretty face, Rachel could guess what had happened.

Angela, for her part, looked sullen and heavy-eyed, and the glances she cast in Rachel's direction were not friendly. Rachel guessed the other girl suspected where Jaime had disappeared to, and Jaime's sudden departure this morning had forestalled any attempt she might have planned to use Robin to make him jealous.

With the Hylton's departure the situation eased a little, and when Liz suggested a game of Scrabble, they all agreed. It was quite a cozy scene beside the sitting-room fire, Rachel reflected, with the gray winter's afternoon closing in around them, but with Jaime gone, they all seemed to feel it in their own peculiar ways.

For her part, Rachel was trying very hard to view what had happened objectively. It was easy to tell herself that now that Jaime had gone, she could relax and enjoy herself, but somehow it didn't come off. With Christmas Day over, and another five days to fill before New Year's, she didn't think she could stand the inactivity, and she found herself struggling for words to explain why it would be better if she went back to London.

Liz herself grew strangely withdrawn as the afternoon wore on, and at teatime she excused herself on the pretext of having a headache. For the first time Rachel glimpsed a certain weariness in her face that had not been there before, and she wondered if Jaime's departure was responsible for his mother's sudden depression. If so, she was glad she had not insisted on leaving straight after her arrival, and conceivably precipitated this mental crisis.

In any event, Liz did not come downstairs again that day. She asked Robert to convey her apologies, and the rest of the family shared a rather silent dinner before having an early night. Somehow, with Jaime's departure and Liz's illness, none of them felt much like being sociable, and when Rachel reached the sanctuary of her room, she felt the weight of what had happened bearing down on her like a ton of lead.

Where was Jaime now, she wondered. From what she had gathered from his father and brother, he was spending tonight in England and flying out to the States tomorrow, and her skin prickled when she considered where and with whom he might be sleeping. Would he go and see Betsy? Was it his usual practice to bid goodbye to her? Or would he spend the night at the apartment, that luxurious penthouse that Rachel remembered so well? Certainly he would have everything he needed there, and be on hand to take a cab out to the airport in the morning.

Rachel undressed and got into bed, and snuggled down determinedly beneath the covers. She could sleep tonight without fear of disturbance, she told herself resolutely, but somehow that thought gave her no satisfaction. It was impossible to forget she had spent the night before in Jaime's arms, or not associate her feelings now with those she had suffered after their separation. Then she had hardly slept for weeks, tossing and turning in her lonely bed, tormenting herself with thoughts of him and Betsy together. It was worse now, after the self-betrayal she was guilty of, and the condemning realization that no matter what she believed she was still as susceptible to his physical appeal.

When Liz didn't appear for breakfast the next morning, Rachel was concerned, and she sought out Robert and asked if there was anything she could do to help.

"Well, I think she might be glad of a few words with you," he said gently, giving her shoulder a friendly squeeze, and Rachel knew a moment's apprehension that seemed totally illogical.

When she entered the Shards' bedroom later that morning, however, her own fears dissolved in her anxiety for the older woman. Liz looked pale and drawn, her hands plucked agitatedly at the coverlet, and she was obviously in some pain. But when she saw Rachel, her warm smile appeared, and she beckoned the girl closer, patting the bed beside her.

"Sorry about this, darling," she said after Rachel had bent to kiss her, and the girl seated herself reprovingly beside her.

"Don't be silly," she exclaimed, patting Liz's hand. "It's you we're concerned about. Now, is there anything I can get you? Robert says you haven't eaten a thing!"

"No, no. I'm not hungry." Liz forced a smile and shook her head. "I'm only sorry this had to happen while you and Robin are here. I so much wanted to keep this a happy occasion."

"It's been marvelous, honestly," Rachel said sincerely. "We've all had a wonderful time."

"Even you? Even Jaime?" Liz looked skeptical. "Oh, if only he hadn't had to leave like that. There hasn't been nearly enough time."

"He'll be back." Rachel tried to sound optimistic, but Liz wouldn't have it.

"He won't. I know it. He's going to America today, and goodness knows when we'll see him again." She sniffed miserably, and Rachel saw to her surprise that she was fighting back her tears. "Oh, Rachel, this was just a wonderful opportunity, and now... now I've flunked it!"

Rachel's wide brow creased. "Flunked what? Oh, Liz, if this has anything to with Jaime and me—"

"It hasn't," said Liz tightly.

"Then what?" Rachel was confused. "Liz, am I being obtuse? I don't understand."

Liz put both her hands over one of Rachel's and held on to it tightly. "Darling, I need your help."

"My help?"

"Yes." Liz's fingers tightened. "There...there's something I should have told Jaime and...and I didn't. You'll be in London when he gets back to England. I...I want you to tell him."

"Oh, Liz...." Rachel moved her head vigorously from side to side. "Liz, I'll do anything for you, you know that, but...but see Jaime! That's something else."

"Why is it?" Liz looked up at her entreatingly. "I thought you two were friends. You...you seemed—well, amicable enough toward one another." Her fingers went slack. "Was that all pretense?"

Rachel could feel her face going red, but fortunately, as the curtains were half-drawn it was not so noticeable. "Well, in a manner of speaking," she murmured now, feeling mean and horribly deceitful. "Liz if there's anything you want to tell Jaime, why don't you call him and speak to him when he gets back to town? You might even be able to persuade him to come up for the weekend."

"No." Liz pressed her lips together. "No, it will be too late then."

"Too late?" Rachel stared at her. "Liz, what do you mean? What is all this? Why have you sent for me?"

Liz sniffed again. "I suppose I should confess everything, shouldn't I?"

"Confess... everything?"

"Yes." Liz seemed unable to meet her eyes. "Rachel, much as Rob and I care for you, we didn't ask you here for Christmas just because we think a lot about you."

"Didn't you?" Rachel felt a faint chill inside. What was Liz trying to say? That she had brought her here because she had known Jaime was coming home? But no! That was impossible. They could not have anticipated his being shot and invalided back to England!

"No." Liz grasped her hand again now with renewed strength. "We wanted to see you, of course we did. You know that. But, well, it was because of Jaime I invited you."

Rachel gasped. "But you couldn't have known—"

"About his injury? Heavens, no!" Liz made a gesture of dismissal. "No, darling, I asked you here because I wanted you to speak to Jaime for me. I was going to ask you to see him after you got back to town."

Rachel was thoroughly bewildered now. "But why?" She shook her head. "You... you must have known Jaime and I hadn't seen one another since—"

"Oh, I know all about that," replied Liz, sighing. "I know you've split up, and everything is over between you, but—" She broke off uncertainly, striving for control. "But," she said again, "I know my son, Rachel. I know he still—well, let's say, he wouldn't turn you away, not if you had something to say to him."

"Meaning you think *I* turned him away when he had something to say to me?" Rachel was stung into retorting, but Liz only shook her head.

"No, darling. No. I'm not criticizing you." She looked up at Rachel gently. "It's not my concern. I can't influence you one way or the other. You...you and Jaime must sort out your own differences. No—this is something personal. Personal to me, that is." She paused, and then said bravely, "Rachel, I've got cancer." And as the girl gazed at her in sudden anguish, she added, "No. Don't look like that. I— I'm not dying. At least, not yet. But I do have to have an operation, and I wanted to tell Jaime before—well, before they operate."

Rachel was appalled. "Oh, Liz—"

"It's a common enough thing, my dear. Lots of women of my age suffer from it. And who knows? The growth may be harmless. They won't know for sure until they can examine it."

Rachel shook her head. "Oh, Liz, you should have told me."

"When?" Liz was practical. "When you arrived? Or on Christmas Eve, or Christmas Day? Which? Darling, I didn't want to spoil the party. I wanted so much for this to be a good Christmas, for all of us. I...I planned to tell Jaime this morning."

Rachel put her other hand over both of Liz's. "Is that what's really wrong with you now? Not your head at all?"

Liz sighed again. "Oh, I have a slight headache, but I think all the preparations have been just a little too much for me. I feel absolutely fatigued and...and Jaime leaving like that—"

"It upset you?"

Liz nodded.

"He wouldn't have gone, you know. If you had told him."

"I know that." Liz shifted restlessly. "But I couldn't come between him and his work. And in any case, I couldn't have told him then. Just like that." She paused. "He looked so tired himself. Exhausted, almost. Did you and he have words the other night?"

Rachel couldn't look Liz in the face, so she bent her head. "Sort of," she murmured, unwilling to elaborate. Then she asked, "But what about Robin? And Nancy?"

"Oh, Robert will tell Robin," said Liz tiredly. "I'm not so concerned about him. He has Nancy, you see. And baby Lisa."

Rachel hesitated for a moment, but it had to be said. "Well, Jaime has Betsy, doesn't he?" she murmured, and winced when Liz's nails scraped her wrist.

"Jaime had no one," she exclaimed fiercely. "He...he and Betsy were divorced over a year ago. Didn't you know about that?"

"No." Rachel quivered. "In...in any case, it doesn't make any difference to us."

"Doesn't it?" Liz looked defeated. "I suppose I was hoping for too much. And I did think you knew."

Rachel pressed her lips tightly together. "Liz—"

"Will you tell him?"

Liz was not making excuses any longer. She just wanted an answer, yes or no, and Rachel knew herself trapped.

"When...when is he due back?"

"I think he said he'd be away for ten days," said Liz tiredly. "That's why I want you to see him. I...I have the operation a week from Thursday. I...I think that's the day he flies home."

Rachel drew an unsteady breath. "What do you want me to tell him?"

Liz's shoulders sagged with relief. "Just...the truth. That...they found a growth inside me, and it has to be removed."

Rachel shook her head. "Where will you be? I mean, where can he get in touch with you?"

"Rob will give him all the details." Liz sniffed again. "Oh, Rachel, I'm so grateful to you."

Rachel wished she felt as convinced Jaime would hear it best from her. After the way they had parted, she was unlikely to be a welcome bearer of news, and she suspected his father would do a better job.

"Liz—" she began again, seeking for words to express herself, but the older woman looked so weary, she didn't have the heart to continue.

"I know you won't let me down, Rachel," she murmured, her eyes closing. "You've got compassion, I know you have. I know you won't break it to him carelessly."

Rachel released herself and got to her feet. She wished she felt as sure of herself and her capabilities. As it was, she felt fearful and apprehensive, and terribly afraid that for all her bland assertions, she was as near to losing her self-respect as she had ever been. The prospect of seeing Jaime again should have meant nothing to her. But it did. *It did!*

CHAPTER NINE

IT WAS GOOD to be back at the apartment again.

After turning up the heat and making herself a cup of tea, Rachel spent some time reacquainting herself with its compact familiarity, adjusting once more to only two rooms and a pint-sized kitchen after the spaciousness of a large house.

But it was a relief to be her own mistress again, to do what she liked, when she liked, and not have to consider anyone but herself. Staying at Clere Heights had been pleasant enough, and she was grateful to the Shards for their kindness, but Jaime's presence had destroyed any sense of normality, and his departure had, in its way, precipitated an even greater insecurity.

Learning about Liz, discovering the secret she had been trying so hard to conceal, had left Rachel with a great feeling of compassion for the older woman. Liz had always seemed so much in control, so competent; to find out she was as susceptible and as vulnerable as everyone else was somehow shocking. It made one doubt one's own convictions, created doubts where they had never been before, and alerted one to the awareness of one's own mortality. Life was so short; its happinesses so fleeting; did anyone have the right to deny the chance of happiness to anyone else?

After Jaime's departure, Rachel had wanted to leave, too, but even that would have seemed a betrayal. After all, she had been invited to stay for the week, and now that Jaime had gone, what possible motive did she have for leaving, too? Besides, with Liz just recovering from being unwell, and Nancy too engrossed in her own affairs to take over, Rachel found herself involved in the actual running of the house, relieving Robert of this duty, and therefore giving him more time to spend with his wife.

Robin was told about his mother, of course, but he took the news with characteristic optimism. "If they're operating, they must think there's a good chance," he remarked to Rachel as she was clearing the table after lunch one day. "They can do marvelous things these days. What with radium treatment and therapy and so on. I was reading just the other day—"

"Well, let's hope you're right," Rachel interrupted him dryly, unwilling to enter into speculative discussions of that sort. "Now, could you carry those glasses into the kitchen for me? I think Mrs. Armstrong's waiting to wash up."

Robin grimaced, but he picked up the glasses and made his way to the door. "I hear you've got the job of telling Jaime," he added. "Hell, ma won't leave well enough alone, will she?"

Rachel sighed. "Robin—"

"Well, it's true, isn't it? I mean, Jaime won't thank you for interfering again, will he?"

Rachel subjected him to a cool appraisal. "Won't he?"

"Not if what I hear is true."

Rachel picked up the tray. "You're imagining things."

"Am I?" Robin made no move to go. "And I suppose I imagined that call he made Sunday morning."

"Sunday morning?" Rachel frowned. "You mean... Boxing Day? The day he left?"

"Yes." Robin looked pleased to have aroused her interest at last. "The studios didn't call him, you know. No matter what he said. He called them!"

Rachel moistened her lips. "Why would he do that?"

"You tell me." Robin was overconfident now.

Rachel flushed. "I have no idea."

"No?" Robin studied her hot face for a few moments, and then shrugged. "Oh, well. Maybe he wanted to get out."

"He had a job to do," declared Rachel stiffly, as the full implications of what Jaime's brother was saying became apparent, but Robin only gave her an old-fashioned look.

"He *took* a job," he agreed. "I doubt if it was offered."

Rachel made a determined effort to get past him, and realizing she was carrying a heavy tray, he moved aside. But the damage was done, and although Rachel told herself that she didn't care why Jaime had chosen to leave so abruptly, it made the task Liz had given her that much harder.

Rachel resumed work at the television studios on Monday. It was a relief to get back into a normal routine after her ten days of holiday, and she was glad that the amount of work that had accumulated excused her from any lengthy discussion as to how she had spent the festive season. Her immediate boss, Geoffrey Zimmerman, knew of her association with Jaime, and where she had intended to spend the holiday, but apart from commenting on the news reports of Jaime's being wounded in Masota, he refrained from asking the inevitable question.

Jaime was due back on Thursday, according to Liz's information, and the first three days of the week alternatively flew or dragged, depending on what Rachel was doing. When she was at work, she managed to forget for whole periods at a time what was facing her, but at home in the apartment it was impossible to avoid. In consequence she ate little and slept badly, and by the time Thursday came around, she was sure she looked a hag. There were dark rings around her eyes, her cheekbones protruded sharply, and there was a tightness around her lips that accentuated their vulnerability.

She guessed that Jaime would probably take a morning flight from New York, which would mean him arriving at Heathrow somewhere around nine o'clock. The prospect of arriving at his apartment at ten o'clock or later, depending on his schedule, was not appealing to her, therefore she decided to phone the studios and find out for herself exactly when he was expected there. Liz was having her operation that afternoon—Robert had telephoned to confirm the arrangements—and for all her misgivings, Rachel knew he would have liked his son to be at his mother's bedside when she awakened. If that was not possible, and it didn't seem likely, the least she could do was arrange for him to be told immediately, and if that meant braving his apartment caretaker at midnight, what reasonable choice did she have?

It was strange dialing the number of the studio where she used to work, and she was relieved to discover the receptionist did not sound familiar to her. It was easier to speak to someone who knew nothing about her, and she gave her name and asked to be put through to Jaime Shard's producer.

"You want to speak to Mr. Shard?" asked the girl, and Rachel tapped her fingers on her desk, prepared to enter into a long explanation as to why she wanted to speak to Max Gilchrist.

"No. He's not there," she explained patiently. "But I have some... personal information for him, and I'd like to find out when he's due back."

There was silence for a while after that, and Rachel guessed the girl was relaying her message to Max Gilchrist's secretary. She wondered if either the producer or his secretary would recognize her name, and then realized uneasily how unlikely it would be if they didn't.

However, when a vaguely familiar masculine voice came on the line, she heaved an impatient sigh. Somehow, she didn't know how, she had been put through to Jack Morrison's office, and through an overwhelming wave of exasperation she heard him asking how she was.

"It is Rachel Williams, isn't it?" Mr. Morrison inquired doubtfully when she made no immediate response, and Rachel forced herself to reply to him, keeping the tension out of her voice.

"I'm sorry, Mr. Morrison," she said in an apologetic tone. "I'm afraid there's been a mistake. I, well, I wanted to speak to Mr. Gilchrist. The receptionist called you in error."

"Is that right?" Mr. Morrison sounded confused. "But— I thought she said you wanted to speak to Jaime." He paused. "He was here a few moments ago, but he's just stepped out for a while."

Rachel was glad she was sitting down, glad too that her position as Geoffrey Zimmerman's assistant provided her with an office of her own. She could hardly believe what Mr. Morrison was saying, and she could feel her limbs responding to the trembling mass inside her.

"Rachel? Rachel, are you still there?" Mr. Morrison was sounding concerned now, and with an enormous effort, Rachel endeavored to respond.

"You...you said...Jaime is—*was*—there?" she echoed.

"That's right. I can get him for you, if you like. I believe he's just along the corridor—"

"No! Wait!" Rachel had to stop him. This was not something she could tell Jaime over the phone. If it was, his mother could have done it herself. And Rachel had promised Liz to break it to him gently. "I, well—" She sought for words. "I thought he was still in New York?"

"New York?" Mr. Morrison sounded bewildered. "But you must know he hasn't been to New York. Pardon me, but didn't you spend Christmas with him at his parents' home in Northumberland?"

Rachel put an unsteady hand to her head. "I—we—he came back to London ten days ago to...to cover an assignment in the United States."

"No." Mr. Morrison was very definite. "Unless he's working for another television company," he added with a dry chuckle. Then he said soberly, "Seriously, Rachel, he hasn't been away since he came back to London last week. If he had, I'd have known about it."

"Would you?" Rachel felt slightly faint.

"I think so." Mr. Morrison was serious now. "Look, Rachel, if there's anything I can do—".

"There's not. Thank you." All Rachel wanted to do now was put the phone down and think about what she had learned. But somehow she had to allay Mr. Morrison's suspicions without him betraying her call to Jaime. "I—well—I wish you'd forget I called."

"Forget you called?" Mr. Morrison sounded perplexed. "You mean you'd rather I didn't mention it to Jaime?"

"Yes."

"Would you like me to arrange to have this call transferred to Max Gilchrist?"

"Oh, no." Rachel was hasty. "That won't be necessary now."

"Very well." Mr. Morrison hesitated. "Rachel, what is it? What's wrong? You can tell me. Jaime and I are—well, friends as well as in-laws."

"In-laws!"

Rachel repeated the word dazedly, and Mr. Morrison gave an impatient ejaculation. "Surely you knew!"

"No." Rachel's hands were trembling so much she could hardly hold on to the receiver. "You mean—you mean you—"

"I'm Betsy's father, yes. Didn't Jaime tell you?"

"No. I—why—" Rachel found it almost impossible to think coherently.

"I thought you knew. I thought he told you," exclaimed Jack Morrison disbelievingly. "But surely when you two split up, he explained the situation then?"

"No. No." Rachel was holding the phone away from her ear now, almost as if by doing so, she was keeping his words from her. "I—I'm sorry. I had no idea. You must believe that."

"It doesn't matter, my dear." Mr. Morrison sounded almost conciliatory. "I'm only sorry you and Jaime didn't make it. He's a good man, and he deserves some happiness."

Rachel gasped. "How...how can you—as...as Betsy's father...say that?"

"Why not?" Mr. Morrison expelled his breath heavily. "I learned long ago that one has to be realistic, Rachel. I fooled myself for far too long."

Rachel couldn't believe her ears. "You mean you *condoned* Jaime...Jaime's—"

"The happiness he found with you?" he interrupted her quietly. "Of course. Why not? It was my fault. Everything that happened was my fault. If I hadn't blinded myself to the truth—"

"Oh, I don't want to hear this!" Rachel couldn't stand any more. "Please. The past is over. It's done with. I...I—just don't tell Jaime I called, that's all. Th-thank you."

She put the phone down then while she still had the coordination of her muscles to do so, and then rested both elbows on the desk as she cupped her face in her hands. Dear God, what manner of man was Jack Morrison to denounce his daughter like that, and what manner of man was Jaime to take advantage of it?

She was shaking so much she felt physically ill, and the

realization that Jaime was here in London, and had never left the country at all, filled her with indignation. How could he deceive his parents like that? How could he leave on some trumped-up assignment without giving them a second thought? Robin was right. There had been no call from London. He had left because it suited him to do so, and she refused to acknowledge that most of her resentment stemmed from the fact that he had evidently wanted to get away from her.

By lunchtime she had herself in control again, and with this control came the realization that if she could contact Jaime now, he might reach Newcastle in time to be with his mother. No matter how unwilling she was to face him again, particularly today after her telephone conversation with Jack Morrison, it was something she had to do, and putting it off could only aggravate the situation.

In consequence, she telephoned the studio again at twelve o'clock, and this time she asked to speak to Jaime himself.

"Who shall I say is calling, miss?" asked the receptionist politely, and Rachel heaved a sigh.

"Miss Williams," she said wearily, and tightened her hand around the receiver.

The silence stretched as she waited for them to find him, and she thought it would be just her luck if he had already left for lunch. But after a few minutes she heard the click as her call was connected, and presently Jaime's attractive voice came on the line.

"Rachel?" he said, and there was an underlying note of...what? Anger? Curiosity? Anticipation? "Rachel, where are you calling from?"

"My office. Where else?" said Rachel flatly. "Jaime, I...I know this is short notice, but...could I see you?"

Another silence sharpened her nerves, stretching them intolerably, making her skin raw and tender to the touch. She could almost feel his mind working, probing the implications of her invitation, trying to anticipate why she might want to see him.

"You mean...this evening?" he said at last. "I, er, I'm pretty tied up at present. But we could have dinner—"

"No. I mean now," Rachel inserted briefly. "I thought we might meet for lunch. I appreciate you're busy, but this is rather...important."

Jaime was clearly nonplussed by her urgency, and she wondered if it would have been simpler just to go to the studio and see him there. But she had wanted to avoid all those faces who had once known her so well, and known of the reasons behind her resignation from LWTV.

"All right," he said at length. "We'll have lunch." He paused. "Do you mind if it's just a bar snack?"

"Not at all." Rachel thought it might be easier in a public bar. And easier, too, to leave once she had delivered her message.

They arranged to meet at the Dragon, a pub midway between his office and hers, and Rachel quickly repaired her makeup before leaving the building. This was one occasion when she wanted to look her best, but she was not very happy with her hollow-eyed appearance. She looked... haunted, she thought impatiently, and then brushed the thought aside as she went to hail a cab.

Jaime was waiting outside the pub, hands thrust into the

pockets of his jeans. A black leather jacket completed his ensemble. It was hardly the outfit for a January day, with lowering skies threatening snow, and a chill wind whipping up the last of the leaves in the park, but he seemed not to feel the cold. He had shed his cane, she saw, though he still favored his left leg as he came to help her out of the taxi, but he had recovered that air of arrogance that she remembered so well.

"Rachel," he said when she was standing beside him on the pavement, looking up into his dark face. Again he said, more thickly, "Rachel!" as he covered her parted lips with his own.

It was an intimate kiss, made the more so by Rachel's involuntary response to it, her quickened breathing promoting an emotional reaction that was both unexpected and unwanted.

"Don't!" she exclaimed, pulling back from him after a moment, her fingers pressed against her lips like some outraged heroine. "I—I—what on earth do you think you're doing?" She saw the anger replace the warmth of passion in his eyes.

With hardening features, he stepped back from her then, the hands that had gripped her shoulders dropping to his sides, his mouth thinning into a narrow line. "Why did you want to see me, Rachel?" he asked without curiosity or expression, and Rachel expelled her breath wearily, feeling completely unequal to the task.

"Shall...shall we go inside?" she suggested, gesturing toward the building, and Jaime inclined his head politely.

"Ah, yes. Lunch," he inferred bleakly. "Of course, we mustn't forget why you came."

"I'll pay for my own," declared Rachel, as they passed through the porch entrance, but Jaime only compressed his lips.

"Just tell me what you want," he suggested coldly, and she ordered a martini and a ham sandwich, not really caring what she ate.

They had managed to find a table in the corner, surrounded on all sides by businessmen and secretaries, all chattering loudly, and filling the air with a cloud of cigarette smoke. It was noisy, but private for all that, and Rachel waited until Jaime had seated himself on the stool beside her before she broached what she had to say.

"I promised Liz I'd speak to you," she said, nibbling at the corner of her sandwich, noticing as she did so he had ordered himself only liquid refreshment. "She—I—well, she wanted to speak to you herself, but . . . with you leaving so unexpectedly—"

Jaime glanced her way. "Didn't you tell her she was wasting her time?"

"Wasting her time?" Rachel was confused. "Why should I tell her that?"

"Oh, come on." He gave her a cynical look. "You know as well as I do what my mother's hopes are, as far as you and I are concerned. Why didn't you just explain that you're so goddamned selfish you don't give a cuss for anyone's feelings but your own?"

"That's not true!" Rachel was indignant. "I care. Of course, I care. I care about your mother."

Jaime looked skeptical, raising his Scotch to his lips and drinking it without pause. Then before she could say anything more, he returned to the bar and ordered himself another one, carrying it back to their table with evident reluctance.

"So...go on," he said wearily after he was seated again. "What does ma want you to tell me? That I should go on hoping when all hope is gone?"

"No!" But Rachel was disturbed in spite of herself. "Jaime...I don't want to quarrel with you."

"Don't you?" His brow quirked. "Why not? Maybe it would clear the air between us? I could do with a damn good row to get rid of your tainted image!"

"Jaime!" Rachel glanced about her anxiously, but fortunately no one seemed at all interested in their conversation. "Jaime, what I have to tell you isn't personal at all. At least, not to me. It's your mother, Jaime. She...she's having an operation. Today."

If the whiskey had given him a temporary release from the problems of the day, her words had an immediately sobering effect. With careful deliberation he set down his glass, and facing her tautly, he said, "What kind of operation?"

Rachel chose her words cautiously. "It's an abdominal operation. To remove a growth—"

"Cancer, you mean?" Jaime was impatient.

"Yes." Rachel nodded vigorously. "But no one knows yet if the growth is malignant."

"Damn!" Jaime raked his fingers over his scalp. "How long has she known?"

"I don't know. Not long, I think. But...she wanted to wait until after New Year's to have the operation. She didn't want to spoil Christmas—"

"My God!"

"That...that was really why she invited me to...to Clere Heights," Rachel went on steadily. "She wanted me to tell you. She...she didn't expect you to be home, you see."

Jaime looked haggard. "I've got to go. I've got to go and see her."

"Yes."

"What time did you say this operation was taking place?"

"This afternoon. I'm not sure of the time."

"So if I caught the early evening flight, I could be with her when she wakes up."

Rachel nodded. "I think she'd like that."

Jaime nodded, too. Then he looked at Rachel. "Are you coming?"

"Oh, no." Rachel moved her head awkwardly from side to side. "I mean, she doesn't need me. She just wanted me to...to tell you. She thought you were away, you see." She paused. "We all did."

Jaime's brows descended. "So how did you find out that I wasn't?"

Rachel sighed. "I called the studio. Your studio. To find out what plane you were flying back on."

"I see." Jaime's mouth was hard. "Well, you can't blame me for that. I thought it was the best thing to do."

Rachel's jaw quivered. "Best for you, you mean."

"All right." He didn't try to deny it. "After what happened I knew I had to get away."

"There was no need." Rachel bent her head. "I could have gone. Your family would have preferred that."

"Did they say so?"

"No. But it's obvious, isn't it?" Rachel's lips were tight. Then she asked, "When... when do you go away again?"

"I don't." Jaime's voice was flat now. "As a matter of fact, Masota was my last assignment. Isn't that ironic?"

Rachel stared at him. "So what are you going to do?"

"Free-lance. Write. Produce that best-seller that's every newsman's dream."

"But—" Rachel shook her head "—can you do that?"

"Why not? I'm not hard up. I can give myself a year at least, to discover what kind of talent I've got. If it doesn't work out, I can always go back to reporting. Or producing. Max says he'll give me a trial if I'm desperate."

"And... and will you stay in London?"

"Maybe. Maybe not." He frowned. "I guess it will depend on how ma makes out." He shrugged. "But if all goes well, I may take a trip to the Pacific. I rather like those islands south of Fiji."

Rachel absorbed what he was saying without further comment. In spite of all her testimony to the contrary, the idea of Jaime leaving London for good filled her with dismay. It was one thing to sever their relationship, knowing he was only the price of a telephone call away, and quite another to accept that, not only would he be out of sight, but also out of reach.

"Well, I guess that's it, isn't it?" Jaime said now, finishing his drink, and Rachel hastily pushed her scarcely touched sandwich aside. "I suppose I should thank you," he added, getting to his feet. "I wasn't very polite, and I should have been."

·"It's all right." Rachel stood up also, stiff and apprehensive, and Jaime's mouth twisted in sudden comprehension.

"Don't worry," he said. "I won't touch you again. This time I know it's forever."

Is it? Is it?

The desperate plea was never spoken, and somehow Rachel managed to follow him to the door. Outside the cold air quickly dissipated any lingering sense of melancholy, and she nodded quite composedly as he bid her goodbye.

"Good luck," he said shortly, and turned away, and had disappeared into the lunchtime crowd before she could make any response.

RACHEL PHONED THE NEWCASTLE HOSPITAL that evening to find out how Liz was, but when she explained she was not a member of the family, only a friend, she was asked if she would call back again in the morning. Rachel guessed the staff were busy and overworked, and were unwilling to supply information to outsiders at such a time, and resigned herself to the overnight wait. Surely nothing was wrong; surely there could be no other reason for their reticence, she consoled herself, but all the same, a small core of anxiety formed inside her.

She thought about Jaime constantly. She thought of the shock the news of his mother's illness had been to him, and the lonely journey north with no one to talk to or share his anxieties with. She should have gone with him, she chided herself tautly, and then dismissed the suggestion and the implications of its inception. What was wrong with her? Was she losing what little self-respect she had left? Whatever happened, her relationship with Jaime was over. But that didn't prevent the realization that she loved him still.

It had crept up on her slowly, this acknowledgment of her own weakness. It had begun the first evening she arrived at Clere Heights, she realized now. She had thought it was compassion, and compassion had been part of it, but it was more, so much more than that impersonal emotion. When he kissed her in the hall after they had fallen among the lights of the tree, she had felt the first stirrings of emotions she had told herself were dead, and the morning he had made love to her she had been angry because she had known how easily he could overwhelm her paltry defenses. Even knowing of his betrayal and the undeniable truth of his marriage, she could not deny her feelings, and the bitter awareness that without him life was just an empty shell.

When he spoke of leaving London she was filled with fear and apprehension. She faced a future secure in virtue, and devoid of all hope. Was that what she was made for? Would she some day regret what she had done? And what did it matter what she thought, when Jaime had accepted it was over, and she did not have the courage to approach him?

CHAPTER TEN

SLEEP WAS A LONG TIME IN COMING that night, and although she must have lost consciousness for a time, she was wide awake when her doorbell pealed around six o'clock. Groping for the lamp on the bedside table, she struggled out of bed, and then hesitated nervously in her nightdress, wondering who it could be.

Her apartment was in a converted house in a quiet backwater near Cromwell Road, and although she shared the building with half a dozen other tenants, she could not imagine any of them coming and waking her up at this hour of the morning. Her milk and her mail she collected from a rack downstairs, and there was no one else she could think of who might come to her door.

The bell rang again, more insistently this time, and as she pulled on a fluffy pink dressing gown, there was a hammering on her door, too, and Jaime's weary voice saying, "Rachel! Rachel, are you in there? Open the door, for God's sake! I have to talk to you."

She didn't stop to put on her slippers, running barefoot across the living room to throw open the door. When she did so, Jaime roused himself from his propped position against the wall, and trudged his way heavily into the apartment.

He looked awful; she had time to register that in those first few moments before he spoke. He hadn't slept, that much was obvious, and there was a night's growth of beard on his chin, and he was still wearing the leather jacket and jeans he had worn to lunch the day before.

"She's dead!" he announced without preamble, and Rachel, who had half been expecting it, grasped the back of a chair for support. "Dead," he repeated, as if he couldn't quite believe it himself. "Isn't that the most bloody thing you ever heard?"

Rachel gestured helplessly toward the sofa. "Sit down," she said, afraid if he didn't he might fall down, and she would never have the strength to lift him. "I'll make some coffee while you rest awhile. I'm sorry I haven't anything stronger, or I'd give it to you."

"Don't you have anything to say?" he demanded, taking no notice of her suggestion. "Don't you want to know how I got here? *Why* I'm here?"

"Of course I do," said Rachel tautly. "And you know I can't possibly tell you how sorry I am. But... but you must rest or you'll be ill, too. You... you obviously haven't slept."

"No. No, I haven't slept," he agreed dourly, but now he flung himself onto the couch to look up at her haggard eyed. "I expect you're thinking I should have stayed with dad, aren't you? Well, he has Robin and Nancy, while I— I—" He broke off then, and buried his face in his hands, "God help me, I needed you!"

Rachel's whole body responded to the need to comfort him, but when she came to sit down beside him, and put her arms around his shoulders, he shook her off like a rabid dog.

"Don't touch me!" he muttered. "I don't need your sympathy! Do you think I'm proud of myself for admitting that I had to see you?"

Rachel drew away unsteadily, her hands clasped together and pressed against her throat. The passion burning in his eyes was like a living thing, the savage emotion of a night in torment.

"Per-perhaps you'd like to tell me what...what happened," she stammered, needing to say something in the face of his violence, and he pushed back his hair with shaking fingers.

"The operation came too late," he muttered harshly. "It was no one's fault. She must have known how the odds were stacked against her. I guess that was why she wanted you to tell me. She knew I might suspect the truth."

"She didn't want you to worry," said Rachel gently. "You know what Liz...was like." It was hard to use the right tense, and her own breath faltered. "How...how did your father take it? I expect he's shattered!"

"Oh, dad will survive." Jaime rested his chin on his fist. "I think he was more prepared for it than I was. I...I was stunned!"

Rachel licked her lips. "Did...did she come around?"

"After the operation, you mean?" Jaime shook his head. "No. They said her heart had failed her. It was quite a major operation. And she's—she *wasn't*—a young woman."

Rachel nodded. "And Robin?"

"Oh, you know Robin." Jaime slumped back on the

sofa. "He cried a lot, and I guess he got it out of his system."

Rachel could believe that. Robin was the type who wasn't afraid to show his emotions. With Jaime it was different. He tore himself to pieces, but inside. Where no one else could see.

"So...how did you get here?" she asked now, trying to act naturally, and Jaime sighed.

"I caught the mail train," he replied flatly. "I told dad I'd fly back later today, but I said I had...things to do."

"And...you came here?"

"It looks like it, doesn't it?" he inquired curtly.

Rachel moved her shoulders helplessly. "I'm glad."

"Are you?" His mouth curled with self-derision. "I'm not sure I am."

"What do you mean?" Rachel allowed her hands to fall into her lap. "You said—you said you...needed me."

"I know."

She hesitated. "And don't you?"

Contempt marked the lean line of his mouth. "What's that supposed to mean? That you'll sacrifice yourself one more time just to appease my grief?"

Rachel caught her breath. "That's uncalled for."

"Is it? Is it?" He pushed himself up from the couch again as if he couldn't bear to sit near her. "Well, relax. It wasn't for your body I came here. I came...I came because I needed someone to talk to, someone who had known ma, who had cared for her. And—all right, I've always found your company...sympathetic."

Rachel looked up at him. "Is that all? Sympathetic?"

Jaime's eyes darkened. "What do you want me to say?" He turned aside from her, slightly dragging his wounded leg across to the screened fireplace. "What kind of confession do you want from me?" he demanded. "That I loved you— more than I thought it was possible for one person to love another; that I wanted you, and needed you, and felt like killing myself when you broke up with me? God, you know all this! So don't tease me now!"

Rachel got unsteadily to her feet. "I...I'm not teasing you, Jaime," she said, acting purely on instinct, knowing that this might be—*would be*—her last chance to heal the breach she had created. The feelings she felt, the decision she had unconsciously made, had manifested themselves. She had not chosen the way. It had been chosen for her. And whatever was in the past, she could not deny this man...or herself...the fulfillment they could only find together. "Does that mean you don't love me still?"

Jaime glared at her across the width of the room. "Love dies," he said brutally. "Without care and nourishment, everything dies!"

"But...has your love died?" she persisted huskily, and his jaw tensed angrily.

"What do you want of me, Rachel?" he grated. "I've done everything I could to show you how I felt. But you don't want me, you don't need me! You've got your apartment, your career, your tidy little life—"

"It's not enough!" said Rachel tautly. "I...I've discovered. It's not enough."

Jaime looked at her through eyes dark with suspicion. "What am I to glean from that remark? That you've decided to make a change? That you've met someone you are prepared to share your life with?''

Rachel nodded. "Maybe."

"So why the hell are you asking me?'' he demanded savagely, crossing the room toward her in three painful strides, taking her by her shoulders, and shaking her until her hair was a tangled mass around her shoulders. Then, and only then, did he seem to come to his senses, and with a groan of anguish, he gathered her close against him. "Don't tell me,'' he muttered, burying his face in the scented hollow between her shoulder and her neck. "Don't tell me about some other man. Not now. Not today. I . . . just don't think I can stand any more.''

"Oh, Jaime!'' Her arms slid around him, beneath his jacket, against the heated skin that seemed to burn through his shirt. "There is no *other* man,'' she told him, choking. "It's you! It's always been you. Only I was too proud to acknowledge my weaknesses!''

Jaime's fingers gripping her upper arms were unknowingly painful. "What?'' he breathed hoarsely. "What are you saying?''

"That I love you. That I want you. That I need you,'' she confessed, cupping his stubbled chin between her hands. "Oh, Jaime, I know it. I've been such a fool!''

Jaime was shaking. She could feel it through her fingers, she could see it in the unsteady stance he was adopting. "This . . . is . . . pity!'' he said tautly. "You're only saying this because you feel sorry for me!''

"No.'' She shook her head, trying to move closer to him, but impaled by his fingers. "Jaime, I'm sorry about your mother, you know I am. And if there was anything I could do to make it easier for you to bear, I would. But," she sighed, "this is you and me Jaime. This is our life! And if you still want me—"

"If I still want you," he groaned, pulling her close to him then, pressing her face against the thudding beat of his heart. "Oh, Rachel, I've never stopped wanting you. You know that."

He kissed her then, deeply and passionately, but without hunger, the sealing of a spiritual as well as a physical relationship. But then weariness got the better of him, and he sank down onto the sofa again with her in his arms.

"You must go to bed," she said, snuggling against his shoulder, and then sat up again at the ironic sound he made. "No," she said, "I mean you must get some rest. You can't fly back to Newcastle in this state."

"Will you come with me?" Jaime's eyes caressed her.

"To Newcastle?"

His lips twisted. "Where else?"

"If you want me to."

"If I want you to," he echoed. "My darling, I want you with me always from now on. Day and night." He paused. "You will marry me, won't you? This is for keeps."

"If that's what you want."

"It's what I want," he agreed. "It's what I always wanted." He hesitated. "About Betsy...."

"Not now," said Rachel, laying a finger across his lips. "You can tell me about Betsy later. Right now you must get some rest, and I must get ready for work." She smiled. "After I've made you breakfast, of course."

Jaime stilled her as she would have left him. "And...Betsy's pregnancy?"

Rachel's shoulders sagged. "If you tell me you weren't responsible, then I believe you," she said simply, and he relaxed.

"I was not responsible," he repeated flatly.

Rachel bent her lips to his. "I'm sorry. Will you forgive me?"

"There's nothing to forgive," replied Jaime, returning her kiss with interest. "Now...go make some coffee, before I lose my good intentions."

RACHEL LEFT JAIME sleeping in her bed, and went to work with a lighter heart than when she had left it. Liz's death was a terrible tragedy, and she would be badly missed, but she couldn't help thinking how pleased Jaime's mother would have been to know that their differences had been resolved at last. Rachel determined not to think of Betsy anymore. She and Jaime were divorced. Their relationship had been over before Jaime sought her company, and if her father was to be believed, she had not been a good wife to him.

But whatever her faults, Rachel couldn't help thinking about Betsy later that morning when a call came through to her from Jack Morrison at London Westward Television. He had never telephoned her before, and apprehension feathered like a butterfly's wings across her skin as she answered his polite greeting.

"I expect you're surprised to hear from me, aren't you, Rachel?" he commented as an opening gambit, and Rachel had to confirm that she was. "Well, after I spoke to you yesterday, I thought about our conversation, and I decided that perhaps I ought to explain a few things for myself.''

"Oh, really, Mr. Morrison, that's not necessary—"

"I think it is," declared Mr. Morrison firmly. "I'd like you to have lunch with me, if you will."

"I can't." To Rachel's relief, it was true. She had arranged to leave work at lunchtime that day, and she and Jaime were flying to Newcastle in the late afternoon. There was no way she could have lunch with Jack Morrison without arousing Jaime's suspicions, and that was the last thing she wanted to do now.

"Are you afraid of me, Rachel?" Mr. Morrison was asking now, and quickly she denied it. "Then why can't you have lunch with me?" he inquired. "I assure you it is rather important."

Rachel sighed. "Jaime's mother is dead," she said without preamble. "We—Jaime and I, that is—are flying north this afternoon."

"I see." There was a moment's silence, and then Morrison said, "I thought Jaime flew up yesterday."

"He did. But he came back again." Rachel sighed. "Oh, I'm explaining this badly."

"I assume you mean he came back to tell you."

Rachel bit her lip. "In a manner of speaking."

"And you're going back with him?"

"Yes." Rachel hesitated a moment, and then said, "I suppose I owe it to you to tell you, Jaime...Jaime and I are going to be married. We...we decided this morning."

"I see." Mr. Morrison sounded impressed. "Well, I can't say I'm not relieved. He looked pretty bad yesterday."

Rachel uttered a nervous laugh. "Thank you."

"And Betsy?"

"Wh-what about Betsy?"

"He has told you about Betsy, hasn't he?"

"Mr. Morrison—"

"Hasn't he?"

"He will." Rachel moistened her lips. "It's not important."

"I think it is."

"Mr. Morrison, yesterday you said you approved of Jaime's behavior—"

"Oh, I do," Mr. Morrison was very definite about that.

"Then why should the question of Betsy arise?"

"Because—oh, because I doubt Jaime, being the man he is, will tell you the whole story, and you—being the girl you are—will always... wonder."

"Not necessarily."

Mr. Morrison sighed. "Rachel, listen to me. I understand how you feel, believe me. But believe me also when I say you wouldn't be human if you didn't have doubts."

Rachel shook her head. "What do you want to tell me, Mr. Morrison?"

"Meet me and you'll find out." He paused a moment, as though consulting his watch, and then said, "Look, it's nearly twelve now. Meet me for a drink if you won't have lunch. Surely you can spare me thirty minutes of your time."

Rachel slumped in her chair. She didn't want to go. She didn't want to meet him. She didn't want to hear about Jaime's relationship with Betsy. But she was also practical enough to realize that there was an element of truth in what Mr. Morrison said. The reason she didn't want to talk about it was because she was afraid.

"All right," she said at last in a tight voice. "I'll meet you in fifteen minutes. But not for a drink. I'll meet you in the park. We can talk more easily there."

"As you like."

The arrangements were made, and Morrison hung up, and Rachel got up jerkily from her desk. She wondered if she should call Jaime and tell him where she was going, and then decided against it. He would find out soon enough. She would tell him. There was no way she was going to start her married life with deception. She had had enough of that.

Jack Morrison was waiting by the bridge where they had arranged to meet. He looked much as usual, bluff and hearty, and with a gruff gentleness, that had endeared him to the girls in the typing pool.

"Shall we walk?" he asked, and she fell into step beside him, hardly aware of the biting wind, and the occasional flurries of snow that market their solitary progress.

"So," he said at last, "how much has Jaime told you? I assume you know about Pollendale."

"Pollendale?" Rachel shook her head. "What is that?"

"Pollendale. In Buckinghamshire. Where Betsy lives."

"Oh. Oh, yes." Rachel nodded. "Yes. I know about that."

"Good." Mr. Morrison sighed. "Now—where to begin." He frowned, and then thrusting his hands into his coat pockets, he said, "I suppose I should start at the beginning

when Betsy was a teenager. She was always a problem child.
Always getting into scrapes. And when she got involved
with a rather undesirable group of young people, it was only
a matter of time before she got involved with the drug
scene.''

"Drugs?" Rachel arched her brows in surprise. "Your
daughter was a drug addict?"

"Was? Is? Who knows?" Mr. Morrison heaved a heavy
sigh. "Does anyone ever really get free of something like
that?"

Rachel's initial apprehension was reluctantly giving way
to sympathy. "You mean . . . she hasn't?"

"I don't know. She's supposed to be cured, but sometimes there's that look in her eyes—" He shook his head.
"But anyway, I'm getting ahead of myself. In the beginning, I thought differently. I really believed that if I could
get her away from those young dropouts, she'd change—
really change, I mean. That's where Jaime came in."

"Jaime?" Rachel's apprehensions stirred again.

"Yes." Mr. Morrison nodded. "He was working at the
studio, of course, and he and I got along well together.
Thankfully we still do. He used to work in features, you
know, before he got involved in current affairs, and I think
he shared my concern over Betsy. She was attracted to him,
I knew that, and when he started dating her, I was really
delighted. Can you imagine? She actually gave up seeing
those long-haired louts she'd been running around with and
she seemed almost . . . normal again. I encouraged their association. I don't deny it. And I sometimes wonder if Jaime
would ever have got as far as marriage if it hadn't been for

me. But, there, whatever the truth of that, he did marry her, and it was a disaster.''

Rachel swallowed convulsively. "Why?"

Mr. Morrison shook his head. "Oh, because she was still hooked on drugs. She'd managed to conceal it from me, her father, but she couldn't conceal it from her husband.''

"I see." Rachel was appalled, but she tried not to show it.

"I doubt if you do," Mr. Morrison said now. "Until you've lived with an addict, you can have no idea how foul being deprived of the drug can make them. They had terrible rows, *terrible*! And Betsy did some terrible things." He paused. "She had always been—how can I say it—fond of the opposite sex. Unfortunately I never realized how fond.''

"You mean...there was another man?"

"Another man?" Mr. Morrison's lips twisted bitterly. "There was a stream of other *men*! Jaime never knew when he went on his assignments who he was going to find in his bed when he got back." He sighed. "Believe me, it's not easy for me to tell you these things. She is my daughter. But I know Jaime, and I owe him so much. And I also know you would never hear the more sordid details from him.''

"Oh, Mr. Morrison!"

He brushed her sympathy aside, and went on heavily, "Of course she was killing herself. Anyone could see that. Her health was failing, and she started hallucinating. She was taken into hospital.''

"I had no idea." Rachel hesitated. "When...when she came to see me, she blamed Jaime.''

Mr. Morrison nodded. "I know. Jaime told me about that. He was shattered when you refused to listen to him. I think he was near to suicide at that time.''

"But...he was still living with Betsy," Rachel protested. "She told me. They had the house in Buckinghamshire."

"What house?" Mr. Morrison looked perplexed.

"Pollendale. You mentioned it yourself."

"My dear Rachel, Pollendale is a psychiatric hospital! I thought you knew. Betsy has been there for the last...five years!"

"But...how could she be? She came to see me—she was pregnant!"

"Pregnant, yes." Mr. Morrison's mouth tightened. "One of the other patients, I'm afraid. A nasty business!"

Rachel gasped. "But how did she get to London?"

"She walked out. She hit one of the nurses over the head and stole her clothes. She can be violent at times. Sometimes I wonder if she'll ever come out again."

Rachel could hardly take this in. "But she had her marriage certificate," she cried.

"Oh, yes." Mr. Morrison was matter-of-fact. "She is allowed to keep her own things."

"But me! How did she find out about me?"

"How do you think? Jaime told her, of course. He wanted her to agree to a divorce. To begin with he was advised not to broach the subject, but she had seemed so much better, and he thought—"

"Oh, God!" Rachel wanted to die of shame and contempt for her own selfishness in jumping to conclusions. Even her father had said that things were not always what they seemed. He had been so right, and she so wrong.

"Anyway—" Mr. Morrison cleared his throat now "—it seems you're beginning to understand why I didn't reproach Jaime over his association with you. I blamed myself, you see. I had...ruined his life. I...and Betsy."

Rachel blinked. She remembered what Mrs. Armstrong had said about Terry Marshall, and how Betsy hadn't been welcome at Clere Heights afterward. She could guess why now. And all she could feel was an enormous weight of depression for the years she had been so unyielding.

"I don't know what to say," she said now. "I'd like to thank you, only I fear that would only seem heartless." She paused. "I...I'm sorry about your daughter, Mr. Morrison, truly I am. But I'm so glad you told me."

JAIME WAS WAITING for her when she got back to the apartment dressed and rather inexpertly shaved with her razor, and pacing somewhat anxiously across the floor.

"Where were you?" he exclaimed as soon as she came in. "I phoned the office half an hour ago, and they said you'd left at a quarter to twelve!"

Rachel moistened her lips. "I did. As...as a matter of fact, Jack Morrison called."

"Jack?" Jaime's brows descended. "Why? What did he want? I didn't know you were in contact with him."

"I'm not. I wasn't. That is—I spoke to him yesterday. When I called London Westward to ask about you." Rachel sighed, as she saw his perplexity. "Oh, darling, sit down and I'll explain. I've got nothing to hide."

Jaime remained standing, and with a little gesture, so did she. "Yesterday," she said, "when I called to ask when you were due back from New York, you had been with Jack Morrison."

"Yes."

"Well—they put me through there. They thought you might still be there. But you weren't. I didn't get to speak to you until later."

Jaime frowned. "Go on."

Rachel linked her fingers together. "He tried to tell me about Betsy."

"I see." Jaime nodded.

"I wouldn't let him," Rachel went on. "I—oh, I was so rude to him. I couldn't believe that he could have...condoned *our* relationship. Not when Betsy was his daughter. I asked him not to tell you I had called, and that was all."

Jaime's eyes narrowed. "And today?"

Rachel bent her head. "He called me. He said he was...concerned about me, about the way I had reacted. I told him that your mother was dead, and that you had come to the apartment, and that we were going to be married, but he insisted I should know about...Betsy."

"And?"

"I met him. And he told me," she said simply, looking at him. "And...and I'm sorry I wouldn't listen to you...before."

Jaime's mouth compressed. "It makes a difference?"

"Of course it makes a difference!" Rachel spoke urgently. "How could you think it wouldn't?"

Jaime shook his head. "I don't know." He massaged his temples with his thumb and forefinger. "So—have you changed your mind?"

"Changed my mind?" Rachel looked puzzled now. "Well, of course I've changed my mind. I...I was a fool. I should have listened to you."

Jaime nodded. "Yes. Yes, you should have done that."
He moved awkwardly toward the door. "I've got to go. I
must go to the apartment, and pick up some clean clothes,
and then get out to the airport...."

Rachel moistened her lips, aghast. "And...and me?"

"I guess you have to get back to work, don't you?" he said
tautly. "Your time isn't your own. I, er, I'll let you know
when the funeral's to be. Perhaps you'd like to come to—"

"Jaime! Jaime, for God's sake, what are you talking
about?"

Now it was Rachel's turn to reach for him desperately,
clutching his sleeve, gazing up at him in pained bewilderment.

"I have to go," he repeated dully, but she wouldn't let
him, hanging on to him defiantly, refusing to believe what
she was hearing.

"Jaime!" she cried. "Are you angry with me? Do you
think I was wrong to listen to what Jack Morrison had to
say? He only did it for you, you know. He knew you would
never tell me...everything. But he did. He did! And, oh,
Jaime, I can't begin to ask your forgiveness for doubting
you so!"

Jaime's lips parted. "You said you'd changed your mind,
that this had made a difference."

"Well, of course I did, and it does! But only because it
made me see things as they really were, not as I believed
them to be."

Jaime grasped her shoulders, bracing himself against the
door frame behind him. "You mean...you mean you still
want us to be together?"

"Do I?" she breathed, the moistness of tears pricking at her eyelids. "Jaime, if you leave me now, I don't know what I'll do!"

"Rachel...." Without another word he pulled her close, silencing her lips with his. Their kiss was intense, passionate, a reflection of the emotions they had both been suppressing. The lean hunger of his body could not be disguised, and Rachel was breathless when he finally leaned his forehead against hers.

"I'm sorry," he said, and when she started to protest, it was he now who laid a silencing finger across her lips. "I mean—I've been a fool," he added. "I thought—oh, I don't know what I thought. When you didn't come back after the receptionist said you had left the building, I could only think the worst. And then when you told me Jack had spoken to you, I finally convinced myself that you had had second thoughts."

"Jaime—"

"I know. It was crazy after this morning, but I'm not in a very confident state at the moment, and I guess I wanted to believe the worst."

"I love you," she whispered, pressing herself closer. "Do you really have to go to the apartment?"

"Yes. But you can come with me," he said huskily. "Right now I think you should have something to eat. You look very pale."

"So do you," she retorted tremulously. "Oh, Jaime, what a day this has been!"

"But at least you know the truth now."

She nodded. "I'm sorry. Sorry about Betsy, I mean."

Jaime sighed. "It wasn't really her fault. She started taking drugs when she was at school, and the outcome was...inevitable."

"He's a nice man—Jack Morrison."

"Very nice," Jaime agreed. "Too nice, as far as Betsy was concerned. She could always twist him around her little finger."

Rachel's lips quivered. "Tell me you love me. Make me feel it. Really feel it, I mean."

"I love you," he assured her softly. "And I'll spend my life proving it."

THE FUNERAL WAS A SOLEMN AFFAIR, and after it was over, Robert accompanied Jaime and Rachel back to London. He was going to stay with friends in Hampshire for a while, and to be on hand when Rachel and Jaime got married in a month's time.

At the apartment Rachel sank down wearily onto the soft leather couch and accepted the drink Jaime offered her with gratitude.

"It's been a long day," she said as he stretched his length beside her, and he slipped his arm around her so that she curled contentedly against his chest.

"It's good to be home," he said, resting his chin on top of her head. "Just having you here makes everything that much simpler."

Rachel smiled. "Simpler?"

"Better, then," he amended. "Brighter, warmer, more satisfying."

Rachel nestled closer, loosening the buttons of his shirt,

and nuzzling her face against his chest. "You smell nice," she murmured, her tongue teasing his body hair, and he put down his drink to gather her closer.

"By the way," he said after he had possessed himself of her mouth, "I have something for you." He slipped his hand into his jacket pocket, and pulled out a scrap of velvet. "This is something I intended to give you more than two years ago."

Rachel's pulses raced as the ruby ring dropped into her palm. It was the ring she had thought had been Betsy's, and her heart leaped as she realized he had intended it to be their engagement ring.

"Will you wear it now?" he asked, without making any attempt to put it on her finger, and with a little gulp she nodded. With great tenderness he slid it onto her finger, and then bent his head and caressed its resting place with ever-increasing ardor.

"So... my mother had her way," he said gruffly, and Rachel pressed her cheek against his.

"I think it was what she wanted," she breathed, and he drew her back to look into her face.

"I know it was," he said quietly. "There was no real reason to involve you in what was essentially a family matter. But she saw an opportunity to throw us together, and her plan worked. However misguidedly."

Rachel stroked his face. "She knew about Betsy, didn't she?"

"Yes."

"She never told me."

"I asked her not to."

"Why?"

Jaime sighed. "I don't know. It seemed my problem, my affair. It was something we had to resolve ourselves."

"And we did."

"Yes, we did," he agreed huskily. Then he added, "By the way, did you mean what you said about being a career woman? I seem to remember you making some assertion about it being better to share one's wife with her work than with another man." He gave her a wry look. "Because I should tell you, I don't think they have television stations in the south Pacific."

Rachel's lips curved. "I suppose it rather depends on the man one marries," she said, her tongue appearing provocatively. "Besides, I didn't say I was a career woman, did I? I was speaking...objectively."

"Well, I'm speaking personally now," he assured her dryly, "and I have to say I'm very pleased to hear it." He yawned, covering his mouth with an apologetic hand. "Let's go to bed."

"I'm...staying here?" Rachel probed teasingly.

"Where else?" Jaime asserted possessively, and she knew there were no more barriers between them.